Pony
Tales

Jade at the Champs

Jade at the Champs

AMY BROWN

HarperCollinsPublishers

HarperCollins*Publishers*
First published 2011
HarperCollins*Publishers (New Zealand) Limited*
P.O. Box 1, Auckland 1140

Copyright © Amy Brown 2011

HarperCollins*Publishers*
31 View Road, Glenfield, Auckland 0627, New Zealand
25 Ryde Road, Pymble, Sydney, NSW 2073, Australia
A 53, Sector 57, Noida, UP, India
77–85 Fulham Palace Road, London W6 8JB, United Kingdom
2 Bloor Street East, 20th floor, Toronto, Ontario M4W 1A8, Canada
10 East 53rd Street, New York, NY 10022, USA

National Library of New Zealand Cataloguing-in-Publication Data

Brown, Amy, 1984-
Jade at the champs / Amy Brown.
(Pony tales ; 2)
ISBN 978-1-86950-843-2
1. Horses—Juvenile fiction. [1.Horses—Fiction. 2. Horsemanship—Fiction.]
I. Title. II. Series: Brown, Amy, 1984- Pony tales ; 2.
NZ823.3—dc 22

ISBN: 978 1 86950 843 2
Cover design by Ingrid Kwong
Cover photography by Steve Bacon
Special thanks to Malabar Riding School
Typesetting by Springfield West

Printed by Griffin Press, Australia

50 gsm Bulky News used by HarperCollins*Publishers* is a natural,
recyclable product made from wood grown in sustainable
plantation forests. The manufacturing processes conform to the
environmental regulations in the country of origin, New Zealand.

Home Sweet Home

You haven't unpacked anything yet!' Jade's dad stood in her bedroom doorway, staring at the stack of untouched boxes. 'What've you been doing for the last hour?'

Jade pointed at the wall behind her, without looking up.

'Yes, I see you've pinned up your ribbons. But your mattress is still covered in plastic — where were you planning to sleep tonight?' Jade didn't answer.

'What are you reading?' her dad asked, more gently.

'Nothing.' Jade snapped the book shut. 'I'll make my bed up now.'

'Good girl. I'll be in the kitchen rinsing that

newspaper-smell off the glasses. You're welcome to join me if you feel like it.'

As soon as her dad had left the room, Jade went back to the book, which was actually a photo album. It was the first thing she'd found in the first box she'd opened, and it had stalled her progress in unpacking. *If I stop whenever I find something that reminds me of Mum or Grandma, I'll never finish*, Jade thought, having one last look at the photograph of herself as a two-year-old sitting in her mother's lap, being read to from Margaret Mahy's *The Lion in the Meadow.*

When her clothes had been folded or hung on coat-hangers and stored in the wardrobe, her bed had been made and her books arranged on the shelf, Jade went out to the kitchen to help her dad. She found him rinsing a wineglass slowly under the hot tap. It seemed to be the first thing he'd managed to unpack, too. Steam curled up around his face.

'Are you OK, Dad?' Jade asked.

He turned off the tap. 'Sorry, Jade, I was miles away. We're not very good at unpacking, are we? Have you made much progress with your room?'

'Almost — that's why I've come to help you. What shall I do?'

Jade's dad had no trouble finding jobs to occupy her for the rest of the morning. Fortunately, a hot nor'westerly wind was blowing, so it was better to be inside in the shade rather than out in the paddock with Pip.

The day before, at the first pony club rally of the year, Jade had tied her reins in a knot, held her arms out straight at each side and jumped Pip, relying only on her legs and seat for control. Flying angels, as the instructor had called them, had been a nerve-wracking exercise of trust, but of course dependable Pip had behaved in a ladylike fashion. Jade's legs were aching today, though, from the extra exertion. She tried to bend and stretch them as she unpacked books and ornaments in the living room.

'Is this a new dance routine?'

Jade turned around and saw that her granddad had let himself in the front door. His fox terrier puppy, Holly, which Jade had given him for Christmas, bounded sideways across the carpet, half-passing like a horse.

'No — I've just got sore muscles from riding yesterday. Hello, Holl!' Jade said, scooping up the puppy.

'Thought we'd pop around to lend a hand. How's your dad doing?' Granddad asked.

'He's unpacking plates and glasses. I think he's OK,' Jade said, and her granddad headed for the kitchen. Jade suspected that her father had started with the kitchen because he couldn't face the boxes of her mother's possessions in his bedroom.

She hadn't gone with her dad to Auckland last week when their old house was being packed up, and she still felt guilty about this. Perhaps if she'd been there, he would have found it easier to give more of their belongings away. Also, the boxes might have been more logically packed. Right now, the one labelled *LIVING RM*, which Jade was sorting through, contained amongst other things chopsticks, books, a desk lamp, a pair of her mother's slippers, photo albums, a game of Scrabble and some old copies of the *Listener*.

It was a time capsule of before the accident. During the last year in Flaxton, Jade could almost ignore that her mother had gone. Mum might have still been living with Dad in the house in Auckland; it was just Jade who had moved. But in the strawberry-pink bungalow, surrounded by their old things and with her dad out of prison, the spell of the last year had worn off.

Jade got up stiffly and went to the kitchen. Her dad and granddad weren't there. 'Dad!' she called, wandering down the hallway, poking her head into rooms.

She found them in the master bedroom. Her dad's eyes were bloodshot and he was trying to smile at her.

'I've almost finished the living-room boxes. Can I go for a ride now?' Jade asked quickly, needing to get out of the house despite the weather.

'We're deciding what to do with Mum's stuff,' her dad said, in a voice that embarrassed Jade. 'I think you should help me with this before you visit Pip.'

The rest of the morning dragged. It was worst when Jade's dad tried to lighten the mood, holding up a purple dress and saying, 'We'd better keep this for your school ball.' All Jade could do was smile weakly. The familiar smell was too much. She wanted to get outside and groom Pip, or even do the dreaded but necessary job of pushing the wheelbarrow around the paddock and using a shovel to clean up Pip's droppings.

'Look, shall I take this pile here to the Salvation Army now?' Granddad asked, wanting to get the job done. 'I could pick up some lunch from the bakery, too.'

By the time Granddad had returned, with brown paper bags of filled rolls, steak-and-onion pies and custard squares, Jade and her dad had finished the hardest part of the job.

The three of them, with Holly trotting between them and licking up crumbs, sat on a picnic blanket under the walnut tree in the backyard.

'It's cooled down a bit now,' Jade said, swallowing the last bite of her filled roll. 'Would you mind if . . .'

'No, off you go. You've been a great help this morning.'

At the Whites' place, Jade parked her bike in the usual spot against the shed and called out, 'Pip! Ready for a ride, girl?'

The large black pony with four white stockings raised her head and snickered.

'Hi, Mr White!' Jade waved. He was in the back paddock, hammering number-eight wire along the top rail of the fence.

'Hi, Jade,' he replied, after spitting out the staples he'd been holding between his teeth. 'Naughty Brandy won't stop crib-biting; she's nearly chewed right through this fence, so I'm taking action. I haven't the heart to make her wear that collar anymore; it was rubbing the back of her neck something awful.'

Brandy, a 16.1-hand bay mare that used to belong to Mr White's daughter, had retreated to the far corner of the paddock and was gnawing at a fence post.

'Such a bad habit,' Mr White said, shaking his head. 'She'll happily suck on the fence instead of grazing or eating her feed — that's why she's losing condition.'

'This one certainly isn't,' Jade said, throwing the lead rope over Pip's solid neck, sliding the halter over her nose and buckling it at her cheek.

'No, she's in fine fettle,' Mr White agreed. 'If it weren't for the rigorous exercise regime you're giving her, she'd get tubby.'

After a swift but thorough grooming, Jade saddled Pip and mounted. The old black pony was unusually skittish in the warm wind. During her last three rides Jade had practised showjumping, and Pip was expecting more of the same.

'She looks half her age,' said Mr White, packing up his hammer, staples and coil of wire. 'You planning to jump her again?'

'I was going to,' Jade said, without looking at Mr White; she was concentrating on keeping Pip at a collected walk rather than a loose jog. 'I wanted to try jumping with no hands again, but she's too full of beans today.'

'The ground's very hard at the moment,' Mr White said. 'I'd give the old lady a day off. Why not take her for a ride around the block?'

'Are you sure we won't get out of practice?' Jade asked, letting Pip break into a trot and guiding her in a large figure of eight. 'The trials are only two weeks away now.'

'You've jumped her three times this week. If you do any more practice, Pip is liable to get sour or lame. Just relax and enjoy a road ride for a change.'

Jade needed no more persuading. Mr White, who had taught her to ride the year before, knew what he was talking about.

Out on the wide grass verge, Jade let Pip have her head. Leaning forward slightly, as if she were beginning a cross-country course, Jade cantered Pip to the end of Station Road and turned right. It was a Sunday, so the traffic was very light. Turning onto Long Road, Jade brought Pip back to a brisk walk.

'No one would think you were nearly twenty-four!' Jade said, grasping a handful of mane as Pip shied at a pheasant darting out from under the poplar windbreak. 'Settle down, miss.' Jade stroked her pony's tense shoulder and pushed her own heels down even further.

Skirting the main street, Jade continued down Long Road, watching out for rabbit holes. At Grove Road, they turned right again and trotted past a small, scrubby paddock of goats, sheep and one skinny cow. Nearly a year had gone by since Jade had passed this paddock and first seen Pip.

'You don't want to go back there, do you, lovely?' Jade said, patting Pip again, and wondering if the pony recognized her old home.

About 50 metres past the pound, Jade turned into Lennox's Auto Repairs, which was also her granddad's house. She and Pip were thirsty, but the back door was locked.

'He must still be helping Dad unpack,' Jade told Pip. 'Shall we just head back to Mr White's now?'

Pip appeared to agree with this suggestion, so Jade, checking carefully for cars, steered Pip across the road in the direction of home. On the last leg of the journey, Pip pricked her ears and whinnied out to a familiar figure up ahead.

'Andy!' Jade called to her friend, who was jogging along on her young roan mare, Piper. 'Nice ride?'

'Not bad,' Andy called, attempting to halt her pony. 'Pip's looking almost as fresh as Piper.'

'Are you alright after yesterday?' Jade asked, loosening Pip's reins as she relaxed, walking next to her friend.

'Yeah, just got a bruise the shape of Australia on my hip. Except for that one buck, I think Piper went pretty well, though.'

During the flying-angels practice at pony club, Piper had thrown Andy.

'Do you think you'll still try out for the Champs?'

'Of course. Probably don't have much of a chance, but it's all good practice.'

'If you'd like to practise with Becca and me on Tuesday, Mr White's giving us a lesson.'

'That'd be great. This is where I turn off for home,' Andy said, crossing the quiet road. 'See you on Tuesday morning, then?'

As Jade rode Pip into the Whites' driveway, she heard an unfamiliar voice, then saw a skewbald horse cantering up and down the long paddock.

'What's going on?' Jade asked, dismounting and leading Pip over to the trough.

'Jade, this is Lisa.' Mr White introduced a young woman with white-blonde ringlets. 'And that's her horse, Floyd.'

Jade and Lisa shook hands. 'Do you graze your horse here, too?' Lisa asked.

'Um, I suppose so,' Jade said uncertainly, not sure whether all of Mr White's generosity could be counted as just grazing.

'Cool! I guess I'll see you soon then.' Lisa got into her friend's white Honda City and drove slowly out the gate without another word.

'You didn't say you were grazing a new horse,' Jade said to Mr White.

'That's because I didn't know until just now.' Mr White looked weary. 'Apparently Lisa phoned when I was out, and Ellen, who can't say no in such situations, told her she could bring her horse around whenever she liked. I wish she'd warned me.'

Jade sluiced the sweat marks on Pip's back, stomach and face, then used a scraper to flick off the white, salty water. When Pip was clean, Jade turned her out in the front paddock. She sat on the fence and watched as her pony walked twice in a circle, then pawed at the dust and sank onto her side to roll.

'I think I could watch horses rolling all day,' Jade

said wistfully, making Mr White laugh. 'Pip looks so happy.'

'She does indeed,' Mr White said. 'I hope Lisa is as attentive to Floyd's happiness as you are to Pip's.'

They both watched the skewbald gelding sniffing at Mr White's big old horse, Hamlet, and Brandy over the fence.

'He looks nice, though, eh?' Jade said, running her eye over his muscular neck, straight legs and rounded haunches.

'Yes, but he doesn't seem to have any tack, just that ratty old halter.'

'Lisa led him here?' Jade asked, surprised. 'Where had she come from?'

'I don't know.' Mr White said. 'I don't know anything about her, and I'm not sure that I like having a strange horse in my paddock.'

Mrs White emerged from the back garden in time to hear Mr White's complaint.

'I'm sorry I forgot to tell you, Jim. I shouldn't have offered grazing without letting you know, but she sounded so desperate. And she says she's planning to sell the horse, so he won't be here very long.'

'She's planning to sell him?' Mr White asked, incredulously. 'Ellen, that means he could be here for months. For all we know she might have dumped him here.'

'For real?' Jade said, aghast. 'Floyd's too nice for that, isn't he?'

'Do you have her phone number, or know where she lives?' Mr White asked Mrs White.

'Oh dear, I didn't ask. I thought she'd give you her details when she brought the horse around.'

'For heaven's sake!' exclaimed Mr White. 'Do you even know her surname?'

Mrs White looked anxious. 'Possibly Jones? I'm sorry, Jim.'

Mr White picked a strand of grass and started chewing on it. 'Never mind, what's done is done. And I suppose I ought to learn to be less suspicious.'

Mrs White and Jade looked at each other. If there was one thing Mr White wasn't, it was suspicious. A suspicious person wouldn't offer free grazing and the loan of tack and riding gear to an eleven-year-old he'd never met before, which is exactly what Mr White had done for Jade a year ago.

'I'm sure Lisa will be back tomorrow and that everything will be alright,' Jade said unconvincingly, as she hopped on her bike.

'I like your optimism,' Mr White said.

Jade biked quickly back to her new home, the strawberry-pink bungalow, thanking her lucky stars that since their Auckland house had sold her father was now able to pay Mr White for Pip's grazing. At least she wasn't as suspicious as Lisa.

Back to Basics

It was nearly five o'clock when Jade biked through the gate to her new home. The late-afternoon breeze felt like a hairdryer, and Jade thought that nothing would taste better than a glass of cold, fresh water. In the kitchen, she found her dad bundling up the last of the packing rubbish. Holly was sprawled on the deck, fast asleep in the sun.

'Was Pip good?'

'Yeah; full of beans, though,' Jade said, gulping down water.

'Granddad's just popped out to fill the gas bottle at the service station — thought a barbecue might be easier tonight.'

'Yum.' Jade suddenly realized how hungry she was after spending the afternoon subduing a skittish pony. 'Could I invite Laura and Becca around?'

'If you like, so long as they don't expect much more than bread, sausages and salad.'

With the new cellphone her Dad had bought her after the sale of their Auckland house, Jade texted her school friends.

Laura, who now lived only five minutes' walk away, texted back that she'd be around soon. Becca, who lived on a dairy farm a few minutes' drive from central Flaxton, replied that she couldn't make it, but would see Jade at Mr White's on Tuesday for their showjumping practice.

Having a quick shower and changing into shorts and a T-shirt before Laura arrived, Jade felt glad to be almost settled again. She could hear her father swearing softly at the computer in the spare bedroom, which was currently more of a study. Holly was yapping as Granddad's Falcon pulled into the driveway. The bungalow was certainly beginning to feel like home.

'Hello?' Laura's voice travelled up the hallway, and

Jade, with her hair still in a bath-towel turban, ran to meet her.

'That was quick,' Jade said.

'I know — it's so great that we live near each other now. These are for you and your dad, a house-warming gift,' Laura said, holding out a bunch of roses, jasmine and sweet peas, and a loaf of fresh bread from her parents' café.

'They're lovely,' Jade said. 'You didn't have to bring anything.'

'They're just from Mum's garden — the flowers, not the bread; that's for dinner. Shall we put them in water?' Laura was already peering nosily down the hallway, clearly keen to be given a tour of Jade's new house. Jade obliged, beginning with the kitchen, where the flowers were left, and ending with her bedroom.

'You're lucky to have a window out to the back garden,' Laura said. 'It's a really nice room.'

'It is good to have back all my things from Auckland. I have the best of both worlds now,' Jade said, trying to slide the photograph of her mother under a book before Laura saw it. She wasn't subtle enough.

'Is that your mum?' Laura asked, reaching for the photo.

'Yeah.' Reluctantly, Jade let her friend look at it.

'And this must be you? What a fat toddler!' Laura laughed, making Jade giggle, too. 'You should put this in a frame,' Laura said. 'Shouldn't she, Mr Lennox?'

Jade's dad was walking past the room, but stopped when Laura waved the photo at him.

'Where did you find this one?' he said quietly, not looking up from the photo.

'Just in one of the boxes with my name on it.'

'Laura's right — we should put it in a frame.'

Being one of those people who enjoy talking to friends' parents, Laura began chatting animatedly to Jade's dad.

'Moving house is tiring, isn't it?' Laura said. 'My mum says it's the second most stressful thing in life.'

'What's the most stressful thing?' Jade asked without thinking.

'Organizing a funeral,' Laura said, then blushed and began babbling. 'Prison must have been stressful as well, I guess. Moving house is probably relaxing after all that. Though starting a new job is the third most stressful, and you have to do that soon, too, don't you?'

'Why don't we go and make a salad?' Jade interrupted, trying to stop Laura's embarrassing stream of conversation.

'Good idea,' Jade's dad said, looking more amused than offended. 'I am indeed starting a new job soon, Laura — tomorrow, in fact, and I still haven't sorted out the computer and Internet here. If you girls could make a salad, that'd be very helpful.'

For Jade, dinner couldn't have been much better. Her granddad, a self-confessed dab hand at the barbecue, had cooked sausages and a couple of steaks to his idea of perfection — grey and bloodless — while Jade and Laura had assembled a green salad. Even better than the food, though, was seeing her father with a cold beer and a full plate, finally looking relaxed.

'Do either of you know a lady with blonde, curly hair, called Lisa?' Jade asked her granddad and Laura, breaking the pleasant silence.

'How old is she?' Granddad asked.

'Maybe twenty.'

Granddad and Laura shook their heads.

'Why do you ask?' Granddad asked, helping himself to the last, now cold, sausage.

Jade told them the story of Lisa's unexpected arrival at Mr White's. 'I'm sure she'll be back tomorrow,' Jade concluded. 'Although Mr White's worried that she's dumped Floyd on him.'

'Gosh, what if she has?' Laura said, with such conviction that Jade couldn't tell if she was being sarcastic or not. 'It could be your first story, Mr Lennox: "Woman Abandons Horse".'

Jade's dad laughed. 'I'm not sure if that'd make the front page, even in the *Flaxton Times*.'

Although Laura wasn't as interested in riding as Jade and Becca were, she was very fond of animals and wanted to meet poor, abandoned Floyd. So on Tuesday morning both girls biked to the Whites'. There, they found Mr White rearranging the weather-beaten practice jumps in the front paddock.

'Are you making us a tricky course?' Jade asked,

pleased, as she climbed over the fence with Pip's halter.

'That's the idea,' Mr White replied.

'I hope you don't mind, but I asked Andy and Becca to practise with me today,' Jade said. 'Hello, girl!' Pip had stopped grazing and begun wandering over to her adoring rider.

'Of course I don't mind — the more the merrier.' Mr White grimaced as he dragged a rotting pole. He had nearly reached the jump stands when it snapped in half. 'Rats!' he growled, making Jade and Laura smile at each other.

Andy was the next to arrive, on a beautifully groomed Piper. Jade groomed and saddled Pip quickly, then mounted and joined Andy, walking in a circle around the jumps.

'Piper is looking amazing,' Jade said, surprised. The usually hot-tempered young pony was relaxed, accepting the bit and tracking up. Instead of shying and throwing little bucks, she had her ears pricked and was paying attention to Andy's commands.

'You noticed the difference straight away,' Andy said, delighted. 'It's this new bit that Michaela gave me to try.'

'What is it?' Jade asked, peering at the three rings sitting at the corner of Piper's mouth. Knowledge of bits wasn't her forte, since Pip had never needed anything more severe than a snaffle.

'It's a Dutch gag,' Andy replied. 'And Piper loves it. I couldn't ride her in a snaffle, because she'd pull too much and I'd lose control, so I used a Pelham. But the straight bar and curb-chain upset her. The gag's good, because inside her mouth it's jointed like a snaffle. In fact, Michaela said that if I buckle my reins through the top ring it would be almost like riding Piper in a snaffle. That's what I want to work up to, so we can finally do a dressage test without running through the rope or kicking the letters over, eh girl? For now, these lower rings give me some brakes.'

'It's a sensible bit for young, strong ponies,' Mr White agreed, gently stroking Piper's nose. 'Shall we see how she goes in it jumping? Becca shouldn't be far away.'

As if on cue, Becca and her nine-year-old dun gelding, Dusty, appeared at the yards.

'Sorry, I'm late,' Becca apologized, dismounting and loosening her pony's girth. 'Carry on without me for five minutes: Dusty needs a drink and a wee break.'

'Did you ride all the way here?' Jade asked. 'I thought your mum was driving you.'

'She was, until we got a phone call from Palmerston. Matthew got kicked by a horse during his practical yesterday and was in hospital last night.'

'That's awful!' Laura said. 'That's why I'm planning to be a small-animal vet — at least cats and dogs can't kick.'

'Where did the horse get him?' Jade asked, trying not to sound ghoulish.

'In the hip, I think. Sounds like he'll be on crutches for a while, but he'll be fine,' Becca said, matter-of-fact about her older brother's injury. 'Mum's made his bed up. I reckon she can't wait to have him home.'

By the time the news of Matthew had been shared, Dusty was refreshed. Becca remounted, and the three girls and their ponies began concentrating.

'Everyone walking in a circle around me,' Mr White instructed. 'Keep a couple of horse-lengths between you and the rider in front. Good. Because we're schooling around the course, the ponies are expecting to jump, but try and maintain a collected walk for now. That's really nice, Andy — I've never seen Piper look so good. Becca, use a bit more inside leg — Dusty can bend better than that. Jade, Pip's falling asleep and your legs are sliding forward. Concentrate, everyone.'

Eventually, when he was satisfied with their walking, Mr White told them to trot. 'Does anyone mind riding without stirrups?' he asked, looking at Andy, who usually had to pass on such activities because of Piper's misbehaviour. 'No? Good. Everyone, fold your stirrups over the pommel of your saddle. We're going to spend the next fifteen minutes improving your seats.'

As soon as Jade stopped using her stirrups, Pip's lethargy left. Jade grinned, pleased with Pip's un-expected extended trot.

'Without the stirrups, you're sitting deeper in the saddle, which is driving her forward,' Mr White said. 'And your legs are in a better position now too. Collect her up just a touch more, so that she's listening to you, then bring her around over these trotting poles. Becca and Andy, follow Jade.'

After everyone had successfully trotted over the poles twice, Mr White asked them to change the rein, still trotting without stirrups, and pop over the criss-cross in the middle of the paddock. 'This is nothing to fuss about,' Mr White said. 'Just keep your pony relaxed and focus on what your legs are doing. When you've popped over the jump, turn to the left without breaking into a canter, and come around on the other rein to do it again. Essentially, you'll be doing a big figure of eight, with a wee jump in the middle. Keep your distance; don't rush. The aim is to encourage your pony to listen to your aids and relax. Don't break into a canter; just let her — or him, Becca — trot. You should each do the criss-cross four times.'

This deceptively simple exercise was exhausting. Making sure not to crowd the rider in front became more challenging as the ponies decided they were in jumping mode and tried to canter. Although the criss-cross was tiny, the lack of stirrups and the repetition made each rider realize her faults.

'Thank goodness that's over,' Becca sighed, stretching her legs after halting next to Mr White in the centre of the paddock.

'How do you feel that went?' Mr White asked, cryptically.

'I think,' Andy said, 'that Piper is finally showing some improvement. I've never jumped her without stirrups before.'

'She was certainly looking good,' Mr White agreed. 'And by the third round, so were you. You'd relaxed just enough, but were still well aware of what your legs were doing. How about you two?'

Jade and Becca looked at each other, wondering who should go first.

'I—' They both said at once, then laughed.

'I reckon I'll be aching tomorrow,' Becca said.

'Why is that?' Mr White asked.

'Because all that trotting and jumping without stirrups made me use a dozen muscles I probably never even knew existed,' Becca said.

'Right, that's exactly what I wanted you to say,' Mr White said. 'Those little-used muscles should really be worked every time you ride. Although your leg position changes when your feet are in the stirrups, your seat should remain just as deep in the saddle and your legs should be working just as hard. What do you think will happen when you ride with stirrups now, Jade?'

Jade was briefly flummoxed. 'Um . . .' She paused. 'They'll feel shorter, because I'm sitting deeper in the saddle?'

'Yes! Exactly,' Mr White said, pleased. 'So, stirrups back now, but remember that basic seat and leg position. In order to improve it's so important to get the basics right first.'

The return to stirrups made the girls feel particularly secure in the saddle. Mr White raised the criss-cross to a 70-centimetre straight-bar and instructed the girls to try the exercise again, except cantering this time.

'It's even more important to keep your distance now you're going faster. Jade, you start. When Jade's over the jump and in the far corner of the paddock, Andy, you begin. Then, when Jade and Andy have both jumped, you start, Becca.'

There were the inevitable hairy moments — Andy and Becca both approached the jump and nearly crashed into each other — but no disasters. When they'd each jumped four times, Mr White told them to bring their ponies back to a walk, loosen their reins and proceed around him in a circle.

'That exercise seems simple and boring,' Mr White admitted, 'but it's a good showjumping warm-up. The figure of eight ensures that the pony gets plenty of opportunity to bend on each rein, and the added challenge of having to negotiate with other riders means that you practise modulating your speed. There's an event at the Champs that involves two riders completing a single course at the same time. That makes this exercise look like child's play.'

The girls looked at each other, excited.

'Right,' Mr White continued. 'You'll see that there's a small course here — nothing over 75 centimetres — but that'll change if you make it through to the jump-off.'

'Just like a competition!' Andy exclaimed happily.

'Yes, that was the idea. Who'd like to go first?' Jade volunteered. 'Right, begin with the oxer in the far left corner, then around to the middle straight-bar. Hang a left, and on to the double, then right, back around to the middle straight-bar again. Last of all, around to the old picket fence.' The old picket fence, with its peeling paint, rusty hinges and rotting wood, was not a favourite of Pip's. Jade kept this in mind as she cantered around, waiting for the 'bell'.

'Ding, ding!' Mr White called, making Laura, who had coaxed Floyd over to the fence and was scratching his forehead, giggle.

Jade and Pip had cleared these fences many times, so, aside from the predictable pause at the picket, their round was clear.

'Nicely done,' Mr White praised. 'Though I'd expect nothing less, this being your home ground.'

Becca, to her embarrassment, had a refusal at the first oxer.

'Take your time to settle Dusty down and try it again,' Mr White said kindly.

'It wasn't his fault,' Becca said, frustrated. 'A pukeko ran out from under the clump of grass by the jump stand just as we were approaching. I hate those birds!'

After getting the starting bell a second time, Becca and Dusty did a good round; slightly too fast due to Becca's frustration and Dusty's excitement, but clear.

'He's a brave jumper,' Mr White said. 'If the course were 20 centimetres higher I doubt he'd even notice.' This made Becca beam. 'However,' Mr White continued, 'you did let him flatten out and race between jumps. If the course had been higher and Dusty had been any less nimble, you would have risked sending poles flying.' Becca's face fell.

Andy, who wished she hadn't had to go last, was struggling to keep her impatient Piper in check.

'You don't have to canter, Andy,' Mr White said. '*Ding, ding!* Just trot up to the oxer; make Piper have a good look at it and figure out her stride, then let her go.'

Andy did what she was told and was pleased with the result. Although their first jump was fairly inelegant, Piper had settled down and listened to her during the rest of the course.

'Brilliant, you're all through to the jump-off, as I'd hoped,' Mr White said, ignoring Becca's initial hiccup. 'Laura, would you mind helping me raise the bars?'

Laura scampered over the fence and assisted Mr White while the girls walked their ponies around to keep warm.

'Would either of you mind if I went first in the jump-off?' Andy asked politely. 'Piper can't stand waiting.'

'Of course not,' Becca said.

Still in a good mood from her second round, Piper jumped well. The new course — without the double, but with a couple of very tight turns around from the oxer to the upright then on to the picket — was designed for a small, agile pony like Piper. Andy, to her surprise, got a clear round.

'I wish I'd timed that,' Mr White said, 'because it looked fast. Becca and Jade, did you notice how, as she was mid-air over one jump, Andy was always looking and steering to the next? This meant that Piper knew exactly what was wanted of her and enabled her to cut all the corners. Well ridden. Walk her around to cool down now, Andy — she's had a great morning's work.'

'What a good pony!' Andy said, patting Piper's sweaty neck vigorously. 'You felt just like a bigger version of Snapdragon then.' Andy's last pony, a nippy 13.2-hand gelding had, amazingly for his size, won 1-metre showjumping classes with Andy before she'd outgrown him.

Becca and Dusty had their round next. As Mr White had predicted, the higher fences posed no problem.

'You could stand to go a bit faster, Becca,' Mr White

said, when they began their cool-down walk.

'I was trying to slow down after you'd told me I was too fast in the last round,' Becca objected.

'Well, there's cantering flat out and then there's cutting the corners and riding cleverly, like Andy. Dusty is very nimble. You can use his flair for games in a jump-off situation. Just trust that if you ask him to bend tightly or cut a corner, he'll be more than happy to do it.'

'OK,' Becca said, crestfallen. 'But he seemed out of sorts today.'

'He was probably a bit tired after the long road ride,' Mr White said, not wanting Becca to feel like she'd ended on a bad note. 'Come on, Jade. Lucky last.'

Aware that, although Pip was good at games too, her size and age meant that she was less nimble than Dusty or Piper, Jade deliberately took the course carefully. It was now a muggy summer afternoon, and Pip, who'd lost focus while waiting for the jump-off, was sluggish. It took all of Jade's energy to get Pip enthused about the first jump. The lazy pony hung her back legs and knocked the pole, although luckily it didn't fall. Less lucky at the picket, Pip, who was now in a foul mood, looked like refusing altogether. Jade gave a little growl and tapped her with the whip about three strides out. This made Pip take off from too far back and knock the rail off with her front legs. Knowing that they were obviously out of the running, Jade decided to collect her pony back and calm her down before the last straight-bar.

'C'mon, girl, don't be like this,' Jade whispered, giving Pip's neck a quick pat as they turned to the last jump. Perhaps because of Jade's encouragement, or perhaps because the last jump faced the other ponies, who were now eating a little of Pip's hay in the yards, the old mare suddenly perked up and cleared it with inches to spare.

'Why couldn't she have done that with the rest of the course?' Jade asked, dismayed, as she walked Pip around to cool down.

'The matron probably objected to having to jump while her friends were resting and eating,' Mr White said, smiling. 'Don't worry about it. You rode well enough, and she won't be in that situation at the try-outs or, fingers crossed, the Champs.'

The Infamous Mr Wilde

Monday, the first day of term after the summer holidays, was hot and cloudy. After wishing her dad good luck at the newspaper, Jade met Laura outside her parents' café at eight, and the two biked slowly to school.

'Guess what?' Laura said as they crossed Flaxton Road. 'Lisa with the blonde, curly hair applied for a job at the café.'

'Really?' Jade asked. 'The same Lisa?'

'She looked just how you'd described her,' Laura said. 'And there probably aren't two Lisas with invisible eyelashes in Flaxton, are there?'

'That's great. Will your parents give her the job?'

'Why is it great? I don't trust her after she just left Floyd with Mr White.'

'It's only been a couple of days,' Jade said, surprised that she was defending Lisa. 'She hasn't done anything wrong. And if she's going to work at the café, that means she'll be staying in Flaxton. She'll have some money to pay for grazing, too.'

'Well, I hope she gets the job and stays because I like Floyd,' Laura said, swinging a leg over her bike and standing on one pedal as she approached the school. 'C'mon, let's see if we're finally in the same class.'

Returning to school after a long summer holiday is never much fun. But, compared with the year before, when Jade was new and everything about the buildings and her classmates was strange, the first day of Year 8 went very well. She and Laura met Becca outside the assembly hall and the three went in together, all crossing their fingers that they'd be in the same class.

As they walked up to the back of the bleachers to find a seat, Jade, just in time, saw a foot stuck out in front of her and stepped carefully over it.

'Hello, Ryan,' she said, rolling her eyes.

'It was worth a try,' he replied, grinning.

'Are you trying to break Jade's ankle before the Champs try-outs?' Becca asked her cousin. 'I guess it's probably the only way you'd have a chance of getting on the team.'

Ryan laughed. 'There are two places in the junior team, cuz. I'll get one of them, and Amanda will get the other one.'

'Amanda?' Jade laughed. 'Isn't she fifteen? She's too old for the junior team.'

'All right,' Ryan said, 'you could possibly get in, Jade, but *she* definitely won't.' He stared evilly at Becca.

'You can't psych me out, Ryan Todd,' Becca said imperiously.

'Quiet at the back, please!' the principal, Mr Rowan, boomed. 'Everyone be seated.'

Throughout the welcome speeches, Jade thought about the impending try-outs. She imagined how Pip would sail over the last fence in the final jump-off — a massive Swedish oxer. They would finish the course in the best time, exhilarated and exhausted, and be guaranteed a place in the team. Ryan, however, would ride too fast at the oxer and get the stride wrong. His pony, Shady, would graunch to a halt, leaving Ryan to clear the fence alone, landing on his bottom on the other side. Jade would graciously refrain from laughing.

'What are you smirking at?' Becca whispered to Jade.

'Nothing!' Jade whispered back. 'Have they almost finished?'

'I think so. He's talking about excelling in every field or something. Have you not been listening at all?'

Suddenly aware that Mrs Crawford was glaring at them, the girls stopped talking and tried to look attentive until finally they were dismissed.

The class lists had been pinned up outside the hall. Laura was the first to find her name. 'Oh, no! I've got Mr Wilde!' she moaned. 'He's *infamous*.'

'Do you even know what that means?' Becca laughed. 'Mr Wilde's fine — he's just really old.

Matthew was in his class ages and ages ago, and said he was funny. I'd swap with you.'

'You won't have to,' said Jade, who'd just found Becca's name. 'You and Laura are in together.' Jade was trying not to sound too disappointed.

'Don't look so emo,' Becca said. 'You're with us, too.'

'Where?' Jade asked, squinting at the page Becca was pointing at. 'I can't believe they'd let us be in the same class!'

'Good morning, young women,' Mr Wilde said as the three entered Room F10.

'Where shall we sit?' Laura asked, meekly.

'Wherever you like, for now. You are now in Form 2 — or Year 8, whichever you'd prefer — so I trust you can restrain yourselves from incessant giggling and chatting.' The girls smiled at each other nervously. 'If I have over-estimated you,' Mr Wilde went on in a voice that may or may not have been serious, 'and you begin cackling like a brood of mad hens, then make no mistake, I will not hesitate to seat each of you next to an undesirable male. Like this chap, for example.'

Malcolm Hodge, a shy boy with dirty blond hair, had just walked in. His face flushed as the girls giggled.

'Let us not waste another minute in which we could be learning,' Mr Wilde said, startling a new group of girls who were walking in. 'Don't look so mousy — you're not late. Please, seat yourselves and encourage your classmates to do the same as they gradually dribble in.' Turning back to Jade, Laura and Becca, Mr Wilde said, 'Just before, I used the phrase "brood of mad hens". What part of speech is the word "brood"?'

The girls were silent. Jade stared at her fingernails.

'Is it a verb?'

'No,' Jade said, 'it's a noun.'

'A collective noun!' Mr Wilde corrected her. 'A brood of hens, a murder of crows, an ambush of tigers. Are you Jade Lennox?'

'Yes, Mr Wilde,' Jade said, surprised.

'I've heard about you from Jim White. Quite the horsewoman, I hear.'

'So's Becca,' Jade said quietly.

'Well then, Becca and Jade: what is a collective noun for horses?'

'A herd?' Becca asked.

'Well, that's the most common of them, yes,' Mr Wilde said, leaving Becca unsure of whether she'd been right or not. 'Better still, you could have answered "harras", "stable", "team" or "troop".'

'A troop of ponies . . .' Jade tried out the phrase.

'No!' Mr Wilde interjected. 'A troop of *horses*. I think you'll find that it's a "string" of ponies. But that's enough wordplay for now. On to the banality of first-day housework. Has anyone seen my register?'

By three-thirty, the girls' cheeks were aching from smiling.

'I still think he's scary,' Laura said to Jade as the two biked home. 'But Becca was right: he *is* funny.'

'I could hardly believe it when he actually pulled out his false tooth and started talking in a Cockney accent!' Jade said, starting to giggle again. 'I think school might be alright this year.'

When they got to the café, Laura persuaded Jade to stay for a hot chocolate. Jade wanted to get home and see how her dad was after his first day at work, but, as Laura pointed out, it would be another hour at least until he'd finished.

'I love Pip's rest days,' Laura said, wheeling her bike around the back of the café to her house. 'It means I get to see you after school.'

'You're always welcome to come and watch,' Jade said, feeling guilty. Although it was hard for Jade and Becca to fathom, Laura just wasn't that excited about ponies and riding.

After the girls had said hello to Bubble, Laura's fox terrier, who happened to be Holly's mother, they found Laura's mum, who gave them each a blueberry *friand*.

'Good first day?' she asked, wiping the table by the window.

'Yeah — we're all in the same class!'

'That's lucky!'

'Very. Could we please have a hot chocolate, if you haven't turned off the coffee machine?'

'Certainly. It'll be good practice for Lisa. You can

tell me later if she's any good at frothing milk,' Laura's mum added quietly, winking.

'She's got the job?' Laura asked.

'Probably. She's on trial for today, learning the ropes. She hasn't any hospo experience, but we're desperate for help and she needs the money apparently.'

About ten minutes later, Lisa brought the hot chocolates to the girls, walking very slowly but still managing to spill the drinks into the saucers.

'I hope they're OK,' she said. 'I put lots of chocolate in to make up for burning the milk.' Laura, who'd been using the coffee machine for years, raised her eyebrows slightly, but Jade thanked Lisa and took a sip. 'It's very hot!' Jade said. 'But otherwise delicious. How's Floyd?'

'Oh, I haven't been around since I saw you there,' Lisa said. 'I'm sure he's fine.'

'He's a lovely horse,' Jade said, silently reminding herself to check Floyd's trough the next day, to make sure he had enough water. 'Where did you get him?'

'A friend up north went overseas and gave him to me,' Lisa said. 'I used to ride ages ago, and I love horses, so I figured it'd be fun to have one again. It's turning out to be a bit of a hassle, though.'

'I go to Mr White's most days after school,' Jade said, slightly sanctimoniously. 'If you need me to do anything for Floyd, I don't mind.'

'Oh, that's sweet of you. He's a bit bigger than your pony, though — more of an adult's horse,' Lisa said, eliciting a cold stare from both girls.

'I bet you're a way better rider than her!' Laura whispered when Lisa had gone out to the kitchen. 'And I'm way better at making hot chocolates.'

As the girls were finishing their *friands*, Jade saw a familiar figure approaching from outside. 'Dad!' she cried, jumping up to give him a hug. 'How was your first day?'

'A bit gruelling,' he said in a theatrical voice. 'No, not really. I think it's going to be a nice little paper to produce. I thought I'd pop in here on the way home to get us a treat to have after dinner, but I see you've already been stuffing your face.'

'I always have room for treats,' Jade said, making her dad laugh.

After Jade and her dad had chosen a piece of chocolate cake and a Neenish tart, they said goodbye to Laura and biked home.

As they turned into Kopanga Road and approached the bungalow, Jade asked her father if he'd noticed the blonde lady who'd given them the treats.

'That was Lisa who keeps her horse at Mr White's,' Jade said.

'Well, you can tell Mr White where he can find her, just in case she's late on grazing payments. How was school?'

From then until dinner, Jade gave her dad a detailed account of Mr Wilde, accentuating his eccentricities.

'Do you have any funny new workmates?' Jade asked, loading the dishwasher.

'Joelene who sells advertising and looks after the classified section is a bit of a dag, but she doesn't have any false teeth, as far as I know, so I think Mr Wilde wins. You'll be visiting Pip after school tomorrow?'

'Yep. And Floyd,' Jade said. 'I told Lisa that I'd keep an eye on him for her, seeing as she's so busy at the café.'

'That's kind of you. Just make sure you're home in time for dinner at seven. I'm going to attempt to make Mum's lasagne and I might invite Granddad over, too.'

On Tuesday afternoon, as her dad had suggested, Jade told Mr White where he could find Lisa. He, too, had noticed that Floyd's water trough had been neglected over the weekend, and he was beginning to worry.

'Well, that's a relief, I suppose,' he said. 'So long as she can balance keeping a horse and a job.'

'Don't worry about Floyd,' Jade said. 'I told Lisa that I'd keep an eye on him for her if she was too busy to see him.'

'Yes, I'm sure that between the both of us he'll be looked after. But we don't want to have our good natures taken advantage of, do we?'

To change the subject, Jade told Mr White that she was in Mr Wilde's class. This cheered him up.

'You're lucky, Jade,' he said. 'Wilde's been saying for the last ten years that he's going to retire, but hasn't yet. He's one of those mythical creatures: a teacher who actually loves teaching.'

Their ride that afternoon — Mr White was exercising Hamlet — was the routine that would be repeated every second day for the rest of the week.

For the first fifteen minutes, Jade schooled Pip quietly at the walk and trot on each rein, concentrating on keeping her tracking up and bending well. For the next twenty minutes, Jade would choose a short course of three jumps, and pop Pip over them. If, after the first round, they went clear, Mr White would raise the jumps a notch or two. Once they'd successfully cleared the course at about 90 centimetres, Mr White would create a new course, using all six jumps, including the double. If Pip was feeling particularly willing, the back rail of the oxer would go up to 1 metre. The last fifteen minutes of the hour-long routine would be a leisurely hack through the orchards at the back of Mr White's paddocks to cool Pip down, who by this stage would be lathered with sweat and jogging like a filly.

With more time in the weekend, the routine was expanded to include agility exercises and intensive schooling. Because the pony club rally had been cancelled that Sunday, Becca and Andy joined Jade at Mr White's again.

Becca turned up first this time. From the yards,

where she'd been polishing Pip's newly shod hooves, Jade could see that it wasn't Becca's mum behind the wheel of the horse-truck, but her brother.

'How's the hip, Matthew?' Mr White asked, as he emerged from the implement shed with a salt-lick.

'The bone's bruised, so it's a bit sore to walk on without the crutches,' Matthew replied. 'But I can drive, so that's good, I guess. Still, it's annoying because we're in the practical module of my course, and I can't do it on crutches so I'm stuck back here.'

While the girls warmed up, waiting for Andy and Piper to arrive, Matthew joined Laura, who was scratching Floyd's star.

'Is this one of yours?' Matthew asked Mr White, patting Floyd's dusty neck.

'No, he's our mysterious boarder.'

'Oh! I like the look of him.'

'He's nice, isn't he?' Laura said — she'd always been a bit in awe of Becca's older brother, mostly because he was a vet student.

'Do you know who he belongs to?' Matthew asked Laura.

'To Lisa, who's just started working at my parents'

café,' Laura said conspiratorially. 'But she hasn't been to see him all week!'

'If I hadn't done my hip in I'd offer to exercise him for her. He looks great,' Matthew said wistfully.

'If you hadn't hurt your hip, you wouldn't be here and wouldn't know about Floyd,' Laura corrected him.

'I didn't know you still rode, Matthew,' Mr White said. 'You must've been about ten and in jodhpur boots when I last saw you at a gymkhana, competing against my Abby.'

Matthew grinned. 'Yeah, I gave up for a while, but since Becca got Dusty, and since I went to uni and met some other people who ride—'

'Other people?' Becca laughed. 'He means Victoria, his girlfriend!'

Laura's face fell slightly.

'Don't be immature, Rebecca,' Matthew said. 'She's just a friend.'

'Anyway, since she's become your "friend", you can't get enough of horses, can you?' Becca crowed.

'Perhaps we should stop gossiping and start jumping?' Mr White suggested. 'Andy's had a chance to warm up now, so, Becca, why don't you do the first round of this course? I've designed it to be difficult; focus on your strides and your turns. *Ding, ding!'*

The course *was* tricky. In the end, Jade and Pip did the best round, but still dropped a rail at the picket.

'Well, Matthew, what do you think our girls' chances are at the trials next Sunday?' Mr White asked in mock seriousness, as the girls dismounted forlornly.

'I hate to say it, Becca,' Matthew said, ready to wind his sister up, 'but I think I'd put my money on Ryan getting in the team ahead of you.'

Furious with disappointment and the frustration that can only be provoked by an older sibling, Becca grabbed a wet sponge covered in horse hairs, and hurled it at Matthew. Even on crutches, he managed to dodge neatly, and it hit Laura smack on the nose. The commotion startled Dusty, who shied and managed somehow to push Becca into the trough, where she sat, still holding her pony's reins, in sopping wet jodhpurs, waiting for Jade to help her up.

'Oh, dear,' Andy said, wiping the tears of laughter from her eyes, 'I don't like our chances much either.'

The Try-outs

The morning of the try-outs was hot and still. Jade woke early, before her alarm had gone off, with her duvet on the floor and her legs tangled in the sheets. In her dream she'd been cantering Pip slowly in a circle around the ring, waiting for the starting bell. As the bell sounded, the reins disappeared and Jade was left with nothing to hold. Steering with her legs, Jade pointed Pip at the first fence. They got the stride right, but in mid-air the saddle disappeared. They landed, and miraculously Jade didn't slip off.

We're going so slowly, we'll get time faults, Jade thought. The jumps seemed to be getting bigger, too. No — Pip was shrinking! As they approached the third fence, a huge oxer, at a shambling canter no faster than a walk, Jade's feet could meet around Pip's girth. Grabbing a handful of mane, Jade tried to steer Pip away from the jump. It was too big — impossible for the shrinking pony. But Pip wouldn't listen. She ran straight at it, then leapt like a cat. Hanging in mid-air, Jade couldn't see the ground on the other side. She and her pony, now no bigger than a Labrador, were nose-diving. *I don't want to land!* Jade thought, and woke up.

Jade's dad was out on the deck with a cup of coffee and two newspapers.

'You're up early,' Jade said, joining him outside with her bowl of cereal and a glass of juice.

'Too hot to sleep in. Will Pip mind the heat today?'

'She'll probably get tired easily. I had a nightmare about her shrinking.'

Jade's dad laughed. 'At least you can be sure that won't happen today.'

'Lots of other things could go wrong.' Jade's breakfast wasn't sitting well in her stomach. She was beginning to wish that she and Pip were going on a leisurely trek instead of to a competition. A farm with some bush and a creek would be nice. She could have a swim while Pip rested and drank.

'You've been working towards this for months — you don't want to pull out now,' her dad said, reading her thoughts.

'Of course not! I'm just nervous,' Jade snapped.

'OK. Fair enough.'

After a quick shower, Jade dressed in an old T-shirt, shorts and sneakers, and checked again the contents of the bag she'd packed the night before: her pristine jodhpurs, shirt, tie, jodhpur boots, white socks, and pony club sweatshirt were all there. Her helmet and gloves were in Mr White's shed with the tack she'd spent two hours cleaning with linseed oil and saddle soap, which was still under her fingernails.

'If you've forgotten anything, send me a text,' her dad called, as Jade hopped on her bike. She was too jittery to kiss him goodbye.

Mr White had already attached the float to the ute,

and was loading Pip's tack into the boot.

'Nice and clean!' he said to Jade, holding up Pip's bridle. 'Abby never kept her tack in such good condition when she was riding. The corner of the brow band was always white with sweat and dust.'

'Thanks for getting everything ready,' Jade said. 'That should be my job.'

'You've still got a pony to groom and plait.'

Pip was down the back of the front paddock, grazing in the shade of the Granny Smith apple trees. Her tail flicked a fly away from her hock, and she looked up with pricked ears as Jade called her name.

In the yard, Jade assembled a bucket of clean water and her grooming kit. She flicked dust out of the body brush with a curry comb, then dipped the brush briefly in the water before rubbing it in firm, massaging strokes over Pip's neck, shoulder, side, back and rump. With her thin, shiny summer coat, and no mud in the paddock, Pip didn't take long to groom.

'Black ponies get such a satisfying shine, don't they?' Mr White said, admiring Jade's work. 'Her legs and feet look OK?'

Jade had checked for heat and lumps in the shins

and tendons, and cracks in the hooves, and fortunately found nothing. 'She's fine,' Jade replied.

'Can't be too careful in this weather,' Mr White said ominously. 'Last night I saw her shifting from foot to foot, but it must have just been the flies annoying her.'

Mr White's pessimism irritated Jade, who was nervous enough without having to worry about Pip's soundness. 'I've decided not to plait,' Jade said sharply.

'All ponies look better plaited,' Mr White replied.

'Not when I've done the plaits. I'll just pull her mane and comb it with water.'

'You're the boss,' Mr White said, 'but you know what Pony Club prefers.'

'I'm not being lazy!' Jade snapped. 'I just think plaits look stupid!'

Mr White stopped himself from laughing, knowing that Jade's nerves were getting the better of her.

'Well, if you've finished sprucing Pip up, pop on her travel sheet and boots, and we'll get her in the float.'

At the corner of Station Road, Jade remembered that she'd left her whip behind.

'I hardly ever have to use it, so it's not worth going back for,' she said. However, as they drove away, Jade worried that this would be the one day she'd need a whip.

'You can borrow Becca's if the worst comes to the worst,' Mr White said, glancing at Jade's tight, pale face. 'Put on that Lulu CD, would you? I think we need cheering up.'

At the pony club grounds, Jade hopped out to open the gate. There were two floats behind Mr White, so he pulled over inside the gate while Jade held it open for the others. In the first was David O'Connor, a seventeen-year-old with a lovely piebald horse. Jade smiled at him and his mum as they thanked her for holding the gate.

Amanda Nisbet and her mother were in the next vehicle. Mrs Nisbet smiled faintly at Jade as they drove past, but neither she nor Amanda said thank you. Over the ramp of their float, Jade saw not the red bay rump of Amanda's pony Aurora, but the blue roan goose rump of a new horse. Although Jade quietly suspected she was a better rider, she was relieved to be competing in a younger age group than Amanda and this new animal.

Jade was about to shut the gate when a huge green-and-white truck, covered in dust, appeared in the distance. Wondering whether she'd feel guiltier shutting the gate on the truck, or making Mr White and Pip wait even longer, Jade dithered. In the end she waited. The driver slowed, and the passenger wound down the window as they passed.

'Thanks very much, Jade!'

It was Michaela Lewis, showjumping team coach and selector, and her daughter, Kristen. Jade beamed with relief. She'd chosen an excellent time to be courteous.

In the grounds, they found a park in the shade, next to Becca's truck. Becca already had Dusty saddled, and was mounting as Jade backed Pip out of the float.

'Am I late?' Jade asked, frowning.

'No, I'm just early,' Becca replied, sounding equally tense. 'Dusty's in a bad mood, and I thought going for a big walk around the grounds might calm him down.' Dusty did a dramatic shy at a plastic bag that was blowing across the paddock. Becca grabbed a handful of mane.

'See?'

Unkind as it seemed, Jade couldn't help relaxing a little, seeing Becca and Dusty just as nervous as she and Pip. *No,* she thought, *Pip isn't nervous.* In fact, she'd been particularly co-operative this morning. Saddling up swiftly, Jade and Pip accompanied Becca and Dusty on their walk. There was still an hour before the trials for the junior team would begin, and Becca's mum had already collected both of their numbers from the registration office, the pony club shed.

Keeping away from the fence line that the pony club shared with the new ostrich farm, the girls attempted to walk on a loose rein, although Dusty was determined to canter sideways, which made Pip jog like a much younger pony.

'This is ridiculous!' Becca squealed, regaining her stirrup after a massive shy. 'What was that even for, Dusty?'

'I think he saw a golf cart through the trees,' Jade said gently. 'Shall we walk in the middle of the paddock from now on?'

'Ostriches booming at us on one side, and golfers hitting balls at us on the other! Has anyone ever complained about how hazardous the Flaxton grounds are?' All Jade could do was giggle. Fortunately Becca started laughing, too. During the past few weeks, pony club members and parents had done little else but complain about the ostrich nuisance.

'I know Dusty would quieten down if I was calmer, but I'm just so nervous,' Becca said.

Jade knew exactly what she was talking about. And so did Andy, whom they soon met at the practice jumps. She was looking pale but determined.

'Did you see that?' she asked in a small voice.

'See what?' Jade asked.

'Good. Piper just refused that straight-bar and I fell straight over her head. It wasn't even a bad baulk — just a naughty I'm-testing-you thing. I wasn't riding confidently enough. Anyway, I just slid off. And your cousin,' Andy said to Becca, 'he couldn't stop laughing.'

'Hubris,' Mr White said, handing Jade and Becca their numbers.

'What?' Andy asked, baffled.

'Hubris,' Mr White said, smiling. 'Arrogance — pride before a fall, so to speak. It's Greek. And it's what Ryan is suffering from. Now, let me hold your ponies while you go and walk the course. Michaela's designed it herself, so it's tough but fair.'

'Oh no — there's a triple!' Becca cried, pointing at the three red-and-white jumps lining the far side of the ring. 'That's the one thing Dusty hates.'

'And it gets worse,' Jade said wearily, once they'd walked the rest of the course. 'The triple's facing the ostrich farm.' The girls all shuddered.

Together, they paced out the strides between the jumps. Jade had learnt from experience that four of her paces equalled one of Pip's strides. Being a very large pony, nearly a horse, Pip usually found doubles and triples tricky. Jade had to really shorten her stride. This time, though, Jade calculated that Pip would comfortably take one stride in between jumps A and B, and two between B and C.

'It's alright for you and Pip,' Becca complained, 'but this is very long for Dusty.'

Andy agreed. 'I wouldn't be surprised if Piper put three strides in between B and C. Three strides and then a sudden baulk when one of those ostriches flaps its wings.'

As it happened, Andy and Piper didn't suffer this fate. On the other hand, Ryan Todd and his pony, Shady, did.

'It's just like you said,' Andy told Mr White, admiringly. 'They were going so well too, until those birds rushed over to the fence.'

'It's a shame for Ryan,' Mr White replied. 'You're right, they were going well; for once he wasn't racing around the course. This will be a challenge for him, though.'

As Michaela's helpers rebuilt jump C, which Shady had skidded into, Ryan tried to walk his agitated pony in a circle. He was stroking Shady's neck and shoulder with his left hand, and still holding a fistful of mane and rein in his right. For the first time, Jade felt sorry for Ryan, and also impressed: most of the pony club wouldn't have stayed in the saddle during that crash; and if they had, some would have blamed their frightened pony, in a nervous rage. No, Ryan had done well to stay calm. Jade silently wished him luck as the bell went and he got a second chance at the triple.

Ryan cantered Shady in a wide circle, giving the anxious gelding a good run-up. As they approached jump A, Shady tried to rush, panicked, but Ryan sat back, deep in the saddle, encouraging his pony to judge the stride correctly, not just run madly. This worked for jump A, but meant that Shady's stride was too short for jump B. Somehow, with an ugly cat-jump, pony and rider managed to make it over, but not without dropping the top rail.

Shady, a brave but inelegant jumper, had remembered the ostriches and was fighting Ryan now. The pony knew what was expected of him, and wanted to perform well, but at the same time was terrified and wanted to get the ordeal over quickly. With the rail from jump B rolling behind him and the impulse to bolt gradually taking over, even his rider's skilful attempts to help him find the right stride couldn't help Shady. Instead of skidding to a halt this time, Shady simply ran straight through jump C, barely even bothering to leap, and hit the top rail with his chest.

'That's eleven faults now,' Becca whispered. 'I can't believe that ploughing straight through a jump gets you the same faults as knocking just one rail.'

'Poor Ryan,' Jade said, watching him struggling to stay in control of his pent-up pony. Now that he was facing the other ponies rather than the ostriches, Shady was really pulling. Jade closed her eyes as Ryan rode full tilt at the last jump, a 1-metre wall painted with red bricks.

'Incredible,' Andy sighed. 'That pony was pretty much galloping, and he still managed to get the stride right and clear the wall.'

'I had to let him have his head in the end,' Ryan said with unconvincing nonchalance as he rode over to the girls. 'It was like we were out hunting.'

Jade wondered why Ryan had come over to them, rather than to his usual friend, Amanda. She looked over and saw Amanda standing with two girls from another pony club. They were all looking at Ryan and smirking.

'I think you rode really well,' Jade said quickly, as Ryan was leading Shady back to the horse-trucks.

'Thanks,' he said, surprised. 'Good luck. You'll need it with those stupid birds over the fence.'

Pip, sensible in her old age, didn't pay much

attention to the ostriches. The only thing bothering her was the heat. With six riders to go before her, including Andy and Becca, Jade found a shady spot and dismounted. Her dad and granddad had just arrived, with a chilly bin of refreshments and two deck chairs.

Jade sucked nervously on a drink bottle and watched another pony and rider make a mess of the triple. 'Will we manage it?' she whispered to Pip, who rubbed Jade's elbow with her nose in reply.

'Do you want some of this?' Jade asked, laughing as she squirted a little water at the corner of Pip's mouth. Most of it missed and hit Jade's dad, who was sitting on the other side of Pip's head.

'For goodness' sake, there's a trough over by the gate, Jade!' he said, wiping the water off his sunglasses. 'Is that Becca riding into the ring now?'

'Oh, yes!' Jade said, crossing her fingers. 'I'm almost as nervous as if it were me in there.'

'Well, it will be soon,' her granddad said helpfully.

Jade grimaced. 'Shh, the bell's just gone.'

'Jade, don't "shh" your grandfather!'

Jade didn't hear, though; her eyes were fixed on

Dusty. He seemed to be in good form: ears pricked, stride confident and smooth.

'Oh, I think they're going to do well,' Jade sighed. 'Look how neatly he tucks his knees up.'

Becca had a fearsome expression of determination as she turned on to the triple. She was clear so far: Dusty hadn't even touched a rail or looked like stopping. With her heels well down and her reins short — a little too short, Jade thought — Becca sat deep in the saddle and drove her pony forward. They met jump A with perfect timing. Pushing her pony more than usual, Becca lengthened Dusty's stride, and he cleared jump B with the same finesse. With the momentum of the first two jumps urging him on, Dusty was so focused on the task at hand that he didn't even notice the strange birds in the next paddock. As he soared over jump C, Jade wanted to clap.

Turning a little too quickly on to the wall, Dusty's hindquarters slipped slightly, and for a horrible moment Jade thought her friend was going to fall. Dusty kept his footing, but was distracted. It was only with a jerking, inelegant hop that he and Becca made it over the wall with no faults.

'That was a clear round!' Jade gasped. 'I'm going to go and congratulate them.'

'You'd better give Pip another go at the practice jump,' Mr White said, legging her up into the saddle and then checking Pip's girth. 'Another two riders and you're on.'

'That was amazing!' Jade said, trotting over to Becca and her mother. 'And after all that fuss you made over the triple when we walked the course.'

'I know!' Becca said, taking off her helmet. Her red hair was plastered to her scalp with sweat and her normally pale cheeks were bright pink. 'It was Mum who told me that if I went into the ring expecting to have problems at the triple, then I'd almost certainly get eliminated. So, as the bell rang, I just gritted my teeth and said to myself and Dusty: We're *going to have a clear round.*'

'If you're not confident, you can't expect confidence from your pony,' Becca's mum said, patting Dusty's neck and looking proud. 'You did well.'

Andy, who was cantering sideways around the ring, waiting for the start bell, looked like she would need more than confidence to get a clear round. The whites of Piper's eyes were showing and her back was up. But, when the bell rang and Andy rode her pony between the starting flags, Piper appeared to relax. She was cantering straight now, and, although she took off from a long way back, she cleared the top rail with at least 10 centimetres to spare.

Becca's mum whistled. 'You can see why Andy puts up with all the theatrics when Piper jumps so well. That pony has a lot of talent, if only she'd settle down.'

'Oh, no!' Becca cried as Piper swerved at the yellow-and-black oxer and ran past it at the last minute. 'Poor Andy.'

'It could be worse,' Jade said. 'At least she kept her seat. I don't think I would've stayed on then.'

Regaining her left stirrup, Andy gave Piper a no-nonsense smack with the whip behind the girth. The pony raced forward, argumentatively, but Andy managed to turn, without crossing their tracks, back to the oxer. This time she kept her legs on and was prepared. Naughty Piper cleared the jump without any trouble.

'I dread to think what will happen at the triple,' Becca said ominously. Fortunately her fears were unwarranted: Piper's agility meant that the long stride didn't bother her, and she cleared the first two without mishap — but graunched almost to a standstill at jump C when she saw the ostriches.

'C'mon, scaredy cat!' Andy growled, urging Piper on. Despite taking the jump from a trot, the clever pony miraculously didn't drop a rail.

With only the wall to go, Andy had relaxed. She let Piper have her head just a touch too much and the pony's stride flattened. Piper took off too far out, and this time caught the top rail with her hind legs and brought it crashing down. Hearing the mistake, Andy's face fell as she cantered through the finish flags. She patted Piper's sweaty neck apologetically and left the ring looking crestfallen.

'Don't look so down! You rode really well,' Becca said as their friend approached.

'Not over the last jump,' Andy replied. 'Such a shame. Except for that naughty run-out and the hairy moment in the triple, Piper was fantastic. I let her down at the end.'

'Don't beat yourself up,' Jade said. 'It shows how good you are that you realize you made a mistake then. Anyway, I'd better go and have a practice jump. We're on after the next pony.'

There was a call over the loudspeaker: 'Could Number 21 please come to the ring. Number 21.'

'That's me,' Jade said, aghast.

At the gate to the ring, a woman with a clipboard explained to Jade that Number 20 had scratched.

'So I have to go now?' Jade asked in a small voice.

'Yes; you're ready?'

'Could I have just one practice jump?'

'Only if you're very quick — we don't want to get behind schedule,' the woman said impatiently.

Panicked, Jade turned and cantered Pip to the practice jump.

'Sorry, can I go quickly?' she said, cutting in front of an older girl on a horse. The girl said something rude, but Jade didn't hear. She cantered Pip at the jump, too nervous to ride well and only hoping for the best. Pip didn't like being rushed. She stopped and knocked the rails down.

'Oh no!' Jade moaned, wanting to cry.

'Look what you've done!' the older girl complained. The practice area seemed suddenly full of unfriendly faces. And now her number was being called over the loudspeaker again.

'I'm sorry,' she said, as someone else's father had to pick up the rails she'd knocked down. 'I'm in a hurry.'

Instead of persisting with the practice jump, Jade patted Pip's neck, trying to soothe herself and her now-tense pony. They walked back together and entered the ring.

'You ready, Jade?' Michaela asked at the truck.

'I think so.'

'OK.' Michaela rang the bell. Jade knew she had thirty seconds to canter around before she had to begin. Trying to forget all sense of urgency, Jade cantered Pip all the way around the ring, letting her look at the ostriches, the wall, the yellow-and-black oxer. When her pony felt happier, she turned towards the flags.

The first jump, a blue-and-white straight-bar, was more inviting than the old, peeling practice rails anyway. Concentrating this time, and doing her best to feel confident, Jade didn't give Pip any reason to baulk. They met the next jump, a red-and-green Swedish oxer, on the right leg and at a good angle.

Jade started to actually relax. 'Good girl,' she breathed.

At the white picket fence, just before the triple, Jade felt Pip falter. *I didn't borrow Becca's whip!* she remembered. *Still, I've got legs and a voice.*

'C'mon!' she growled, and drove Pip on decisively with her legs and seat. It worked. Pip had sensed the importance of the occasion and was performing well.

Unlike the others, Jade was unfazed by the triple. She knew that if she met the first jump at the right stride, the rest would be easy. For once, they were an easy distance apart for Pip. And as for the ostriches, well, they were no match for Jade's mature pony.

In this frame of mind, Jade and Pip looked similar to Becca and Dusty as they approached the triple: determined and successful.

Taking a good look at the three obstacles in a row, Pip slowed but didn't show any sign of stopping. Clearing jump A neatly, B and C were, as Jade had predicted, no trouble at all.

As they landed, clear, over jump C, Jade wanted to make a fuss of Pip right then and there, but remembered Andy's folly. Instead, she restrained her triumphant pony and ensured that the final wall stayed intact as they sailed over it.

'And that's our second clear round,' Jade heard Michaela say over the loudspeaker.

'Only second?' Jade said to Mr White as she slid off Pip's back and ran up her stirrups. 'Only Becca and I have gone clear so far?'

'That's right,' Mr White grinned. 'And there're only three more competitors, so there might not even be a jump-off. If I were a betting man, I'd put money on it that the two places in the junior team have been filled. But we shouldn't count our chickens just yet. And what happened at the practice jump?'

'It was terrible,' Jade said. 'The entry before me had scratched and the lady at the gate said I could have a practice jump, but only if I rushed. So I cantered over, all stressed, and cut in front of someone else. Then Pip actually stopped and all the rails fell down. I should've just taken her into the ring — we were fine in there, amazingly.'

'Ideally, you should've warmed her up a little earlier,' Mr White said.

'But I had to watch Andy!' Jade said, irritated by Mr White's tone. 'Anyway, we got a clear round.'

'I know, I know. You did very well in the end. But with a less patient and good-humoured pony you mightn't have been so lucky.'

'I know,' Jade agreed, chastised.

The next competitor knocked two rails down in the triple. The rider after that forgot the course, and in her confusion turned a circle and crossed her tracks, which meant instant elimination. Jade felt sorry for the girl, who was weeping with frustration as she left the ring, especially when the girl's father started shouting at her.

'You wouldn't shout at me like that, would you?' Jade asked her dad quietly, as they watched the angry scene.

'Of course not!' her dad replied. 'I'm too ignorant to shout — I don't even know why she was eliminated.'

Becca and Dusty stood with Jade and Pip to watch the last rider's round. The afternoon was still and hot — nearly 30 degrees — and neither the girls nor ponies felt like a jump-off. Mean as it seemed, they were all willing the rider to make a mistake.

'They're doing well,' Becca said grimly. The words had barely left her mouth when there was a thunderous crash in the intermediate course, just to the right of the junior ring. A horse had skidded at great speed into a jump, sending poles rolling all over the place. Jade saw it favouring its near foreleg as it left the ring, with a cut on its knee and blue flakes of paint from the jump on its chest.

The commotion had distracted the chestnut mare in the junior ring, causing her to run out at the yellow-and-black oxer. Trying to look sympathetic, but breathing sighs of relief, Jade and Becca led their tired ponies over to the trough. Their work was done for today; it was time for a drink, a feed and a sluice-down.

With the ponies comfortably tied up and feeding from their hay-nets at the horse-float, Jade, Becca, Andy and their various supporters picnicked in the shade.

'I wonder where Laura is?' Becca asked, finishing a sandwich and feeling suddenly like one of the chocolate muffins that their friend had promised she'd bring in the afternoon.

'Maybe she decided it was too hot for a long bike

ride?' Jade said. 'If so, I don't blame her.'

'I feel sorry for the senior riders,' Andy said, gazing back at the third course, which was still in the midst of a jump-off. 'No one should have to ride in this heat.'

'Well, it looks like they've found the winners,' Jade's granddad observed as a cheer went up across the paddock.

'Who do you think won?' Becca's mum asked. 'Who's going to be on the team with you two?'

Jade and Becca beamed, while Andy and Ryan looked crestfallen.

'Surely it'll be Kristen Lewis?' Mr White said, helping himself to another piece of bacon-and-egg pie.

'No, she's turned fifteen,' Andy said. 'That means she's in the intermediate squad.'

'Gosh, I'm glad we weren't competing against her!' Becca said. 'That'd be impossible.'

'Is Amanda the second intermediate rider?' Jade asked Ryan.

'I dunno. Didn't see her round,' Ryan said quietly.

Becca raised her eyebrows at Jade.

'It looks like they're getting ready to announce the winners at the pony club shed,' Mr White said. 'You two had better get over there.'

'Not before you've tidied yourselves up!' Becca's mum cut in. 'Rebecca, your hair is a mess, and Jade, you've got tomato sauce on your cheek. Andy, can you help them look presentable while Ryan and I clear up the picnic?'

At the shed, Michaela Lewis was standing on a hay bale and holding a loud-hailer. The pony club district commissioner, Mrs Thompson, standing next to the tiny Olympian, was nearly at the same height as Michaela, despite standing on the ground — and nearly as loud, despite not having a megaphone.

'Welcome, riders!' she boomed. 'Today we have tested the best young show-jumpers from each of the pony clubs in the district, in order to create a really fine Flaxton team for the New Zealand Pony Club Association North Island Show Jumping Championships. Gosh, what a mouthful!' She paused, and beamed. 'Without further ado, I will invite our local Olympian, of whom we are so very proud, to announce this year's team. Michaela?'

'Before I tell you officially who's in the team,' Michaela said, 'I'd like to say a few things about my course-building.'

'There have been some complaints,' Becca's mum whispered to Jade and Becca.

'In Cambridge, at the Champs,' Michaela went on, 'the courses are tough. They require not just fast or brave riding, but thoughtful, creative riding — especially in the jump-offs. While the jumps might not be as high as you're used to, the distances between them, the angles at which you have to meet them, and the distractions outside of the ring are challenging. In designing these courses today, I tried to prepare you for this. The senior ring had a couple of very tight turns, I know. In the intermediate ring, jump 8 was unusually narrow, which brought some of you to grief. And in the junior ring there was the combined test of the triple and the ostriches. Those of you who managed to get clear rounds under these conditions deserve to be in the team. Now, can we all please congratulate our juniors: Rebecca Brown and Gold

Dust, and Jade Lennox and Pip — Whoops! I mean, Onyx.' Michaela knew Jade's pony by her paddock name rather than the registration name written on the paper in her hand.

Jade and Becca went to the front, slightly embarrassed, as the crowd clapped. 'And,' Michaela continued, 'our intermediates: Kristen Lewis and Dorian, and Amanda Nisbet and Blueberry Tart. Well done, sweetie,' Michaela said, kissing her daughter on the cheek and making her growl *'Mum!'*

'Finally, our seniors, who are fresh from a tiring jump-off: Corina Tawhai on Medusa, and David O'Connor on Toblerone.'

'What a wonderful-looking team!' Mrs Thompson boomed again. 'I'm sure they'll make us proud.'

A Higher Standard

What on earth?' Jade exclaimed, as she unloaded Pip from the float. Mr White turned around and followed Jade's gaze to Floyd. He was standing in the side paddock, calmly grazing, with a saddle hanging under his stomach.

'Thank goodness you're home!' Mrs White said, emerging from the back garden. 'Poor Floyd has been galloping about like a creature possessed. I tried to get his saddle off, but of course he wouldn't let me near him. He's only just calmed down in the last ten minutes.'

'What happened?' Mr White asked. 'Where's Lisa?'

'I've no idea,' Mrs White said, shaking her head.

'I got back from the supermarket and found him like this.'

'If only Brandy and Hamlet could tell us what's been going on,' Jade said. The two placid horses were standing in the shade of the apple trees at the back of their paddock, nibbling at each other's withers.

Swiftly putting Pip in a yard with a bin of hard feed, Jade ignored her gear, which was still in the back of the ute, and instead tried to entice the distressed Floyd over to the gate.

'You go by yourself first,' Mr White told her. 'You might remind him of Lisa.'

As Jade approached the anxious gelding, with a halter behind her back and a carrot held out on her flat palm, she wondered whether reminding Floyd of Lisa was such a good thing. She, after all, had no doubt put him in this uncomfortable position.

Jade was right. Try as she might, making clicking noises with her tongue, she couldn't coax Floyd at all.

'Maybe he's sick of young females?' Jade said, eventually giving up and handing the halter and carrot to Mr White. 'You're the opposite — he might like you?'

Mr White laughed. 'OK, I'll give it a try.' Walking

quietly to a point in the middle of the paddock, Mr White called Floyd's name, gently. 'Here, Floyd. Let's get that saddle off you, eh boy?'

Wiggling his ears and snorting, Floyd trotted in a large circle around Mr White three times before halting, stretching his neck out, sniffing, then finally approaching the carrot.

'Good man, well done,' Mr White said slowly as the suspicious horse ate out of his palm. Jade watched from the gate, stock-still and silent.

Gradually, in three smooth movements, Mr White slipped the lead rope around Floyd's neck, the halter over his sunburnt nose, and the head strap behind his ears. Fastening the buckle at his cheek, Mr White stroked the tense neck.

'Shall I take the saddle off while you hold him?' Jade asked, beginning to climb over the gate.

Seeing the girl out of the corner of his eye, Floyd pulled back violently on the lead rope, burning Mr White's hands.

'No, I think it'd be better if I take him into the yard next to Pip and do it myself. Why don't you unpack the ute?'

Jade nodded, disappointed that Floyd so obviously disliked her.

'I don't take it personally,' she whispered to Pip as she retrieved the now-empty feed bin and scratched the pony's star, sending a small cloud of white hairs floating like dandelion seeds across the yard. 'It's just because I remind him of Lisa, who doesn't know how to handle him. At least you like me, eh Pip?' In answer, the contented pony rubbed her nose vigorously on Jade's shoulder.

'Hey!' Jade laughed, being pushed against the fence. 'If my shirt wasn't already dirty, you'd be in trouble for that.'

As Mr White unbuckled the girth and freed Floyd of the saddle, Pip leant over from the other yard and sniffed at the new horse. Floyd laid his ears back on his head and stamped a hind leg threateningly.

'Easy, boy — enough of that,' Mr White soothed. 'While you're in here I may as well give you a quick groom and put some sunblock on that peeling nose of yours. And look at your cracked hooves! They'd benefit from some Stockholm Tar.'

Jade watched admiringly, from the safe distance of the shed, as steadily Floyd settled down and responded to Mr White's patient handling.

'He likes you,' Jade said enviously, carrying the last of the tack into the shed. 'He looks like a good horse right now.'

'I think he is a good horse,' Mr White replied, gently releasing Floyd's near-hind hoof and straightening up, holding his back. 'He doesn't seem mean-spirited, just poorly handled. It's a shame. I'd very much like to know where Lisa is right now, and where she acquired this saddle. It looks ancient — and if its tree wasn't broken before she put it on Floyd, it certainly is now.'

Mr White wasn't the only one interested in Lisa's whereabouts. First thing in class on Monday, Laura regaled Jade and Becca with the excitement of the weekend.

'You will never believe what happened on Sunday,' Laura stage-whispered, with one eye on Mr Wilde.

'Lisa was supposed to start at midday and never turned up.'

'Is that why you couldn't come to the trials?' Jade answered, forgetting to whisper.

'Yeah,' Laura replied, slightly louder. 'We were really busy and I had to cover for Lisa. That's not all, though . . .' Laura paused dramatically.

'Is the gossip of the weekend so pressing that it can't wait until morning interval?' Mr Wilde asked wearily, not looking up from the papers on his desk. 'I believe you each have a copy of *Oliver Twist* to keep you busy while I collect my thoughts. Or have you been reading so diligently that you've finished it already?'

Jade, who hadn't had time to so much as open the unappealing tome, suddenly felt nervous. Before she could make an excuse, Laura piped up: 'I'm sorry, Mr Wilde, but this is really quite important.'

Peering over his glasses, Mr Wilde looked up in mock interest. 'Oh, but Laura, you should have said earlier. Please, we must all hear this serious news.'

If Mr Wilde had expected Laura to be too embarrassed to speak in front of the whole class, he was mistaken. 'Well,' she said, looking around at her audience, 'a new girl that Mum and Dad employed at the café didn't show up on Sunday, and what's more, the takings from Friday weren't banked. She closed up the shop then, so right now she's the prime suspect,' Laura finished, grandly.

'There's more,' Jade cut in. 'When we got back from the trials, we found her horse, Floyd, in the paddock with a saddle on. It had slipped under his belly.' Suddenly aware that this was an anti-climax after the story of the theft, Jade blushed and started picking at her fingernails.

'How exciting,' Mr Wilde said. 'A villainous girl thieves *and* mistreats horses. Because this piece of gossip was particularly juicy, I won't split you girls up. But, be aware: next time I won't be so lenient. In future, save your nattering for break-time, please.'

Relieved that they hadn't really been told off, but eager to continue chatting, the girls reluctantly opened their copies of *Oliver Twist* and began reading.

The long sentences and strange language caused a dull ache behind Jade's eyes, and Oliver's not having a mother was an uncomfortable reminder of her own situation. Bored with the first chapter, Jade skipped ahead at random. The page she opened to happened to mention a horse. 'The hostler was told to give the horse his head; his head being given him, he made a very unpleasant use of it: tossing it in the air with great disdain, and running into the parlour windows over the way; after performing those feats, and supporting himself for a short time on his hind-legs, he started off at great speed, and rattled out of town right gallantly.' Jade giggled quietly. She doubted that Charles Dickens had ever ridden a rearing horse. Still, the more she pictured the horse 'supporting himself for a short time on his hind-legs', the more accurate the description seemed. She smiled.

'I'm glad you're enjoying it, Jade,' Mr Wilde said with genuine pleasure. 'But I'm afraid I'll have to ask you to put *Oliver* away for now. It's time to go over our mathematics homework.'

Fractions weren't as diverting as *Oliver Twist*, though. While Mr Wilde rabbitted on about one-third equating to 33.33 per cent, Jade wondered what had happened to Lisa.

As soon as the bell rang for morning interval, the girls resumed their conversation.

'Have your parents phoned the police?' Becca asked, opening a packet of corn chips.

'Not yet,' Laura replied. 'They're trying to get hold of her first, to see if she'll give the money back. Mr White doesn't know where she is, does he, Jade?'

'No, but he's trying to track her down, too. I'll be around there before practice this afternoon, so I'll text you if I hear anything.'

Michaela Lewis had wasted no time in organizing the first practice for Flaxton Pony Club's new showjumping team. Usually, even just the thought of it would have given Jade butterflies as she biked to the Whites' after school. But Lisa's disappearance made a two-hour lesson with the district's best young show-jumpers seem relatively trivial.

Before she was even off her bike, Jade asked Mr White whether he'd found Lisa.

'She's gone,' he said simply. 'Ellen found an envelope in the letter box this morning, with a note from Lisa and some money for grazing. That's something at least, I suppose.'

'You know where the money came from?' Jade asked. 'Laura's café! Apparently, instead of banking the takings on Friday afternoon, she stole them. She hasn't been back since, and Laura's parents are trying to find her. Do you think I could read the note?'

Jade followed Mr White into his house, guiltily enjoying the detective work. The note, written on a thin sheet of yellow paper, read:

Dear Mr White
I'm sorry I haven't been looking after Floyd very well.
Here is some money for his grazing. He is yours now
if you want him. If not, I hope it is not too much
trouble for you to find him a good home.
Yours sincerely,
Lisa

'So the grazing money Lisa gave me was stolen from the café?' Mr White asked, wearily.

'It seems likely,' Jade said. 'Hey, you don't think Floyd was stolen too?'

Mr White stared at Jade, aghast. 'Please don't say that, Jade! It'll be troublesome enough trying to sell him on, even if he isn't stolen property.'

'I can ask at practice if anyone wants a new horse,' Jade offered. 'Which reminds me, Becca's picking us up in ten minutes and I haven't even groomed Pip.'

'You'd better get cracking then,' Mr White agreed. 'I'll call Laura's parents now and let them know about Lisa.'

On the way to the pony club grounds, Jade told Becca and Matthew about Lisa's note.

'So Floyd's on the market, then?' he said thoughtfully.

'Would you be interested?' Jade asked. 'You seemed to get along with him the other weekend.'

'Yeah, it's been ages since I rode, but I'd be keen to start again.'

'You should talk to Mum about it,' Becca said sensibly. 'After all, we'd be the ones having to look after Floyd while you were in Palmerston.'

'I'm the one chauffeuring you about today,' Matthew said, elbowing his sister in the ribs. 'I think it'd only be fair if you looked after my horse while I'm away.'

'Only if you let me ride him,' Becca replied.

Matthew took a deep breath. 'I don't know if I could do that to poor Floyd,' he said, teasing. 'The way your hands wobble about when you ride Dusty! I wouldn't wish that on any horse of mine.'

Becca gasped and punched her brother in the arm. The two continued bickering all the way to the grounds. Jade looked on, laughing, and once again wondering what it would've been like if she'd had siblings.

'Girls, you're late to the first practice,' Michaela scolded as they trotted over to the other ponies and riders. 'That's disappointing.'

But once again, on the strength of their gossip about Lisa, the girls were excused.

'Poor Jim,' Michaela said, shaking her head. 'That's a burden. Not to mention the café!'

The rest of the team, and the riders' parents, murmured about the scandal for a few minutes, the general agreement being that such things hardly ever happened in Flaxton.

'That's enough gossiping for now,' Michaela finally

announced, clapping her hands. 'Everyone walking in a circle around me now, to warm up. Kristen, you lead off. Today, what I want from you is humility and attentiveness.' As if on cue, Pip pricked up her ears, making Jade smile. 'You're each feeling pretty great about winning a place in the team — and so you should. However, this is just the beginning. Right now, you and your ponies are good by Flaxton standards, but from hereon in Flaxton standards aren't good enough! I want a higher standard from each and every one of you, OK? I know you're all capable of succeeding, as long as you listen to me.'

At Michaela's command, each of the riders walked, trotted and cantered their ponies and horses, first on one rein and then the other.

'And now, adjust the stride,' Michaela said, in a hypnotic voice. 'Collect the canter, make it shorter, bouncier, full of scope. More, Jade — Pip's canter is still flat. That's better,' Michaela praised, as Jade concentrated on sitting deep in the saddle and driving forward with her seat, while keeping her legs wrapped firmly around Pip's sides.

'On the count of three, I want you each to count

four canter strides, then move back down to a trot. Ready? One, two, three.'

When Michaela was satisfied with the warm-up, she led the team over to a course of three fences, each four strides apart and not quite in a straight line. 'Amanda, Corina and David, keep warming up for now,' she said to the team members who were on horses rather than ponies. 'I'll move the jumps further apart once the ponies have been through.'

The jumps were only 80 centimetres high, but Jade suspected there would be a catch.

Becca looked nervous, too. Kristen, on the other hand, was lying back with her head on Dorian's dapple-grey rump and chewing at the rubber handle of her whip.

'Have you done this before?' Jade asked Kristen.

'Hundreds of times,' Kristen replied in a bored voice. 'I know it's good for the horse and stuff, like a pianist doing scales before playing whole songs, but I'd rather just jump a course.'

'The jumps are on a funny angle,' Becca said.

'Yeah, that's the point,' Kristen explained. 'The first time through, Mum will tell us to approach each jump straight on, and concentrate on getting our ponies bending correctly. The second time through, she'll ask us to canter in a straight line, meaning that we approach the jumps on an angle, if you see what I mean.'

Becca did see, and she was instantly worried. 'That sounds hard.'

Jade smiled at Kristen. 'Becca always complains that something's too difficult, then does it perfectly.'

Becca blushed.

'OK, girls,' said Michaela, who'd been adjusting the height of the last jump. 'This exercise is like scales for a pianist.'

The girls started giggling. 'What's funny?' Michaela asked, looking stern.

'Nothing, it's just that Kristen was telling us about the course and used exactly the same words,' Jade said.

Michaela smiled then, too. 'Goodness! You've actually been listening to your mother's advice. As a reward, I won't make you go first. Becca, how about you?'

Becca made a face, but did as she was told.

'Don't rush,' Michaela said, as Dusty broke into a brisk canter. 'Take it easy, feel for the strides and use your legs to keep Dusty nice and supple as he bends.'

Becca listened carefully and did her best, but Dusty still didn't bend to Michaela's satisfaction. 'That was a good first attempt, but on the last jump in particular, you cut the corner and approached it on an angle, which isn't what I was asking for this time. Come round and try again.'

With a worried but determined expression, Becca did the course again, exaggerating the corners this time and going at a very slow canter.

'Lovely!' Michaela clapped. 'Just what I was after. See if you can do exactly the same, Jade.'

Pip, who was often a little reluctant to bend correctly on the left rein, managed the first two jumps well, but became disunited on the last corner. Although Pip cleared the third jump, Michaela pointed out to Jade that, had the jumps been much higher, they would have been less lucky.

'One more try, Jade,' Michaela suggested. 'This time, left leg firmly pressed at the girth on the final corner.'

Doing as she was told, Jade rode Pip through the

course again, this time with better results. Pip was on the right leg the whole way through and approached each jump straight and balanced.

'That's what I mean by a higher standard,' Michaela said, addressing the horse-riders too, who, bored of warming up, had stopped to watch Jade's round. 'So far, you've all managed to scramble through a small pony club course, on the wrong leg or disunited. From now on, I don't just want clear rounds, but *controlled* clear rounds. Kristen, your turn.'

Although she and her Grand Prix-winning pony, Dorian, had appeared lethargic and bored until now, their demeanour changed as soon as they approached the course. With a firm seat, and almost invisible commands with her legs and hands, Kristen went straight from walk to canter.

'That looked perfect,' Jade sighed as they completed the course.

'Practice makes perfect,' Michaela said. 'It's a cliché, but in this case it's true. Practise this exercise regularly and you'll see a marked improvement.'

Before changing the course for the horses, Michaela asked the pony-riders to go through once again, this time cutting the corners and approaching the jumps on an angle. To demonstrate, Kristen and Dorian went first.

'You put in an extra stride between the last two jumps,' Michaela said critically. 'But we're running out of time, so I won't make you go again.'

When her mother wasn't looking, Kristen rolled her eyes, making Jade giggle.

'Your turn now, Jade,' Michaela said, either oblivious or ignoring the girls' cheek. 'If you ride confidently at the first jump, the rest should go smoothly.'

Pip was dubious of approaching the first jump at an unnecessarily odd angle, but Jade drove her on as if they were beginning a jump-off. This strong start meant that Pip's stride was too long as they met the second jump. Jade collected her pony and managed to get the correct four strides. This careful riding pleased Michaela. 'It's attention to detail like that which will shave seconds off your jump-off times,' she said, before telling Becca to have her turn.

'If you're worried about the angle, pretend it's a jump-off; that's what I did,' Jade whispered to her nervous friend.

Taking Jade's advice, Becca cantered Dusty in a warm-up circle. From his pricked ears and bouncy stride, Jade could see that Dusty had understood Becca's signal. They approached the course in a tight circle, as if it really were part of a jump-off. Realizing what was required of him, Dusty sped up but still made four perfect strides in between each jump. Becca gave him a firm pat on the neck as she trotted back to the group.

'A fraction faster than I'd like to see,' Michaela said. 'But he seemed to be enjoying himself and you were in control, so I shouldn't really complain.'

When Michaela instructed the pony-riders to warm down with a ten-minute walk around the grounds, then untack their ponies, Becca and Jade were disappointed.

'We didn't even do a whole round of a course,' Becca complained to Kristen, as they walked on a long rein, three-abreast, around the cross-country course.

'Yeah, exercises aren't that much fun,' Kristen agreed. 'But if you look at your pony,' she gestured at Dusty's damp belly, 'you'll see that he's been working hard.'

'I guess,' Becca said.

'That was quite fun, though,' Jade said, trying to lighten the conversation. 'I feel like I learnt something.'

'That's lucky,' Kristen said. 'At the end of every lesson she takes, Mum makes you tell her what you've learnt.'

Sure enough, once the team had met at the pony club shed — on foot this time, having made their hard-working mounts comfortable at the trucks — Michaela asked everyone to share what they'd learnt.

Becca, to Jade's surprise, went first. 'I learnt that even though that exercise seemed small compared with doing a whole course, it was actually really hard work for Dusty.' Kristen raised her eyebrows at Becca and then started laughing.

'First of all, I don't know why you're all so giggly — I'll excuse it as team bonding —' Michaela said, 'but, yes, Becca's absolutely right. What seems boring and repetitive to us can actually be a challenging gymnastic exercise for our horses. Think about it. Alright, who's next?'

Jade wished she'd got in next, because everyone

else ended up saying, in slightly different words, what she'd learnt. When it came to her turn, Jade mumbled, 'Just the same as everyone else, I suppose: the importance of controlling your pony's stride in between jumps.' Jade blushed as she finished. Speaking in front of people, especially older, better riders than herself, was never easy.

'Can't be repeated too many times,' Michaela said. 'Controlling your horse's stride improves your chances of getting a fast, clear round. Simple as that. Showjumping is technical. It's about getting your timing and angles right. Both of these rely on a correct, controlled stride. I know this practice was a bit boring, but I hope you understand its importance. Next week I promise we'll apply what we've learnt today to a real course.'

By the time Jade had said goodnight to Pip and let her go in Mr White's front paddock, it was eight-thirty and nearly dark. She biked home quickly, hungrily wondering what her dad had made for dinner.

As she let herself in the front door, Jade's dad was

on the phone in the hallway.

'Jade! Where have you been? Why weren't you answering your cellphone?' he said, hanging up the receiver as he saw her. His eyes were wide and panicked.

'Just at practice,' Jade said in a small voice. 'Sorry if you were worried.'

'Have you lost your phone?' he said, almost shouting.

'No, it was just at the bottom of my school bag. I forgot about it.'

'I thought you'd had an accident — Mr White didn't know where you were, Granddad hadn't seen you. I was about to call the hospital.'

'I'm fine,' Jade said quietly, embarrassed. 'Sorry I didn't check my phone.'

'Never mind,' her dad said, giving her a tight hug. 'I don't know what I'd do without you, Jade.'

Jade didn't know what to say. 'What's for dinner?' she asked eventually, still trapped in the bear hug. Her dad let go of her and chuckled.

'Yes, I guess you're starving. Get changed out of your riding gear and I'll heat up the macaroni cheese.'

Sitting on the couch with her dad, watching *CSI* on the TV and shovelling her dinner into her mouth, Jade felt pleasantly weary.

'How was your day?' she asked her dad during an ad break.

'Pretty good,' he replied. 'We've decided to run a story about your friend Lisa and the disappearing café money.'

'She's not my friend!' Jade objected.

'I know, I was just teasing. Anyway, the story will be printed tomorrow. Readers who have any information on Lisa's whereabouts will be asked to phone the Flaxton police station.'

'It's got serious,' Jade said, suddenly feeling some sympathy for the young, blonde woman who couldn't look after her horse.

Poor Pip

In response to Jade's dad's story in the *Flaxton Times*, the police and local radio station were inundated with supposed sightings of Lisa. Joan, Granddad's friend who ran a tiny second-hand book shop, thought she'd seen a woman fitting Lisa's description standing outside the Salvation Army chapel as if she were waiting for someone.

'This was last Sunday morning at about seven,' she said, cheeks pink and eyes twinkling. Jade and her grandfather had been birthday shopping for her dad and were walking down Flaxton's main street when Joan had called out to them.

'Me, I'm an early riser,' Joan went on, clearly

delighted to be able to contribute first-hand to the town's mystery. 'So, as I was doing a little dusting out the front of the shop, I remember seeing one of those nasty little boy-racer cars. You know the sort: shiny and low to the ground, exhaust pipe as wide as this vase.' She held up a large white china object, with a milkmaid and a cow painted on its side. Jade thought the milkmaid looked like she was about to cry and couldn't blame her.

'Yes, I know what you mean,' Jade's granddad said impatiently.

'Well, the girl Lisa — I'm sure it was her — hopped into this car and they drove off north.'

'What did the driver look like?' Jade asked.

'You know, I couldn't tell you. The windows were tinted.' Joan shared this last detail with relish, as if it revealed more about the driver than a description of his face ever would.

At school a girl from Year 9 came over to Laura at lunchtime and told her that she knew how she felt.

'What do you mean?' Laura asked, baffled.

'Two of our sheep have gone missing, and my brother saw someone with blonde hair running along the fence line the other night. We reckon it must be Lisa.'

'Oh,' Laura said. 'Um, thanks for letting me know.'

'No problem,' the girl said seriously, before joining the queue at the tuck shop.

'This is getting ridiculous,' Becca said, when the girl was out of earshot. 'Lisa couldn't have stolen two sheep. I saw her — she's scrawny as, and sheep are heavy.'

'I don't know,' Laura replied darkly. 'I wouldn't put anything past her.'

After another few days of speculation, during which the police established that Lisa wasn't with her parents and sister in Palmerston North, the mysterious blonde woman became a missing person. Jade's dad's stories weren't just published in the *Flaxton Times* but in the *Dominion Post*, too.

Seeing her photo in a North Island-wide newspaper must have been the last straw, because the day after the story was printed, Lisa came forward to a police station in Hastings.

'She'd run away with her boyfriend, but felt terrible when she realized her family thought she was dead or something,' Laura told the class and an indulgent Mr Wilde. 'She phoned Mum, and has already started to pay the money back, so we're not going to press charges,' Laura added.

'So the local drama has finished its season?' Mr Wilde said to his confused class. 'The curtains have closed and we must return to the monotony of everyday life?'

'I guess,' Becca said uncertainly. 'Mr White owns her horse, Floyd, now, so that's her last connection with Flaxton gone.'

During the week-and-a-half of Lisa's disappearance, Matthew had been visiting Floyd regularly. Although his hip injury was still healing and riding was out of the question, Matthew could hobble into the paddock with pockets full of horse mints and spend half an hour making a fuss of the abandoned horse.

Not bothering with a halter, Matthew would take a body brush into the paddock and, as he chatted to Floyd and fed him treats, groom him thoroughly. It wasn't long before Floyd was following Matthew around the paddock like an obedient dog.

'That's amazing!' Jade said one afternoon as she watched Matthew playing with Floyd. She'd just finished a good hour's exercise and was cooling Pip down by walking on a long rein. Kicking her feet out of the stirrups and stretching her tired legs, Jade watched Matthew tell Floyd to 'halt'. He then hobbled about 10 metres away, stopped and said, 'Come, Floyd!' On Matthew's command, the young gelding trotted over to the person with the pockets full of horse mints. Briefly rewarding Floyd with a treat, Matthew proceeded to walk in a figure of eight, with the horse shadowing him, nuzzling at his pockets.

'If your mum saw that, she wouldn't be able to resist letting you have him,' Jade said.

'That's the idea.' Matthew grinned.

The following weekend, Becca, Matthew, their mum

and Dusty all came to Mr White's in the truck. Although Becca had insisted that she just wanted to practise jumping with Jade, Becca's mum smelt a rat.

'The abandoned horse?' Becca's mum said, when Matthew admitted that he was keen to take Floyd. 'I thought he was barely broken in. And anyway, when did your interest in riding return?'

'Floyd and I get on well. Wait and see.'

With an audience of his mother, Mr White, Becca and Jade, Matthew performed a little show with Floyd. By speeding up and slowing down his own walking pace, Matthew could make Floyd to follow him at a walk or trot, on command.

'Very good!' Mr White laughed, clapping as Matthew took a little bow then hugged Floyd's neck. 'That's just what he's needed — a bit of fun to help him trust people again. He's yours for free if your mum agrees.'

Everyone looked at Becca's mum. 'Oh, for heaven's sake, alright. We'll take him. I was worrying about trying to push an unbroken horse up the ramp of the truck, but it looks like he'll follow you anywhere, Matthew.'

However, when Becca and Jade had finished their practice and the time came to coax Floyd onto the truck, the task wasn't as simple as Becca's mum had predicted. Floyd baulked, then spun around as soon as he heard the hollow sound of his hoof hitting the wooden ramp.

'Careful of your hip!' Becca's mum shouted as she watched Matthew, who was holding Floyd's lead rope, get pulled down the ramp.

Although he was clearly in pain, Matthew was patient with Floyd. He spoke quietly to the trembling horse, leading Floyd away from the truck until he was calm enough to have his neck and shoulder stroked.

Without saying a word, Mr White came over to Floyd with the bum-rope and started patting him too. Unflustered, he eased the big loop at the end of the rope around the horse's hindquarters and threaded the long end through the ring of the halter.

'There, now,' Mr White said gently. 'You ready for another try, Floyd?'

Becca, who had been waiting inside the truck with a now agitated Dusty, looked worried as she watched her brother approach the ramp again.

'Be careful!' she shrieked. 'Dusty's panicking.'

'He's only panicking because you're shrieking like a banshee. Calm down,' Matthew hissed.

Jade and Becca's mum were on either side of the ramp, acting as barriers just in case Floyd dashed to one side. Mr White was standing behind at a safe distance, ready with the lunging whip, and Matthew had Floyd's lead rope in one hand and a horse mint in the other.

'C'mon, mate — good boy,' he pleaded to Floyd, who'd walked right to the bottom of the ramp but was going no further. Wincing as he bent down, Matthew gently picked up Floyd's near foreleg, and placed the hoof quietly on the ramp. Moving to the horse's off-side, he did the same to the other hoof.

Frozen with nerves, Floyd stood stock-still, two hooves on the ramp, two on familiar ground. Everyone was clicking their tongues and making cajoling noises. Even Dusty, probably out of frustration rather than encouragement, had started whinnying. Every creature nearby seemed to be willing him to get onto the truck, and eventually Floyd stopped dithering. With a nervous leap that nearly bowled Matthew over, the young horse charged up the ramp and joined Dusty.

'Well, that could've taken a lot longer,' Becca's mum said, bolting the truck door. 'At least getting him off shouldn't be such a problem. And you, young man, are going to spend the rest of the evening with your feet up. You're limping badly.'

'I'm fine,' said Matthew, trying not to wince as he hoisted himself into the passenger side of the truck.

'How's Floyd getting on without Matthew?' Jade asked Becca, as they warmed up their ponies together at the fifth and now second-to-last showjumping team practice.

'He's a bit heartbroken, I think,' Becca replied. 'It's been three days since Matthew went back to uni, and Floyd's already worn a track along the fence line of his paddock. He won't stop neighing either. It's quite sweet really, except that he seems to hate me and Mum as much as he loves Matthew. Dad has to get his cover on and off and chuck him his biscuit of hay.'

'Maybe Lisa put him off girls for life,' Jade said.

'Stop chatting now, ladies,' Michaela called. 'Come into the centre and I'll tell you what we'll be doing this afternoon.

'Today, it's a competition,' Michaela continued, when the whole team was gathered around her. 'We're going to have a go at the Jigsaw event. Who can tell me what that involves? Corina?'

'Um,' said the shy seventeen-year-old, 'is that the one where two of us have to go around a course at the same time?'

'Yep,' Michaela agreed. 'Spot on. Say you have a course of ten jumps, like this one here, you each must clear five jumps. The idea is for both of you to complete the course and go through the finish flags as quickly as possible, which means you have to be tactical. I'll hold your ponies now, while you walk the course I've set up. Walk it in pairs, keeping in mind your own strengths and weaknesses. For instance, Amanda, your horse, Blue, is bigger than Kristen's pony, so you'd leave the really tight corners to them. Make it as easy for yourselves as possible.'

'Pip doesn't mind picket fences, does she?' Becca asked Jade as they wandered around the course together, measuring strides by their walking paces as they went.

'Only the ugly one at Mr White's.'

'Good, in that case, you can do the wall and the picket.'

'Getting from the picket to the wall is really tight!' Jade complained. 'Unless we take the long route around the double, but that would waste time.'

'And you might get in our way as we do the double,' Becca added, seeing the problem. 'This is tricky.'

'How about we do the picket, the blue oxer, the double and the red upright?' Jade said eventually. 'That way, we'll be going as fast as we can around the outside of the course, while you do the tight, twisty angles in the middle.'

'That still leaves me with the wall,' Becca whined.

'Dusty baulked at that wall once, six months ago, and you've cleared it fine ever since. Stop being a wuss.'

'That's enough time!' Michaela yelled. 'Mount up now, everyone. Jade and Becca, you'll go first, before I raise the jumps for the others.'

The girls trotted around the ring, careful not to get

in each other's way, and waited for Michaela to ring the old pony club bell.

When she heard the bell, Pip broke into a canter. Jade steered her through their start flags and they were off. After successfully clearing the picket, they nearly collided with Dusty and Becca who were approaching the green-and-white upright.

'Sorry,' Jade squeaked, pulling Pip back almost to a halt, then urging her on again when the path was clear. Pip was unimpressed with this erratic riding, and appeared to seriously consider running out the side of the blue oxer. If Jade hadn't had her left leg firmly on and her sternest growl at the ready, they might have got three faults. But, as it was, Pip grudgingly cleared the oxer and cheered up as she cantered flat out around to the double on the other side of the ring.

Four strides away from the first jump in the double, Jade collected Pip's canter. Pleased to find her pony on the correct leg and feeling willing, Jade grinned as they cleared both jumps A and B. With only the red upright to go, Jade once again let Pip have her head. As they charged towards the last jump, Pip's stride was a bit flat. She took off from too far back and caught the top rail with her shins. Hearing the clunk of the pole hitting the hard ground, Jade's face fell as they cantered through the finish flags.

'Sorry!' Jade apologized to Becca as they left the ring.

'I'm sorry, too,' Becca replied. 'We knocked a rail as well.'

'Great first attempt,' Michaela told them, patting Pip's neck as they halted next to her. 'You know what you did wrong, Jade?'

'Went too fast at the end,' Jade said, crestfallen.

'Yep, with uprights especially, you have to get Pip's stride short and bouncy. If she's cantering flat out, she'll misjudge the jump's height. When you have enough space between jumps to give Pip her head, by all means speed — time is of the essence, after all. Just make sure she's collected in time to meet the jump correctly. You did that well before the double.'

Jade nodded at this advice.

'Same goes for you, Becca — although you had a bit of bad luck with that rail falling. I barely heard Dusty touch it.'

While Becca held Pip's reins, Jade helped Michaela raise all the jumps in the course to 1 metre, ready for Amanda and Kristen's round.

Kristen, who'd competed at the showjumping champs as a junior the previous year, was familiar with the Jigsaw event and had quickly chosen a sensible course each for her and Amanda.

'I honestly think that this is our best bet,' Kristen said, for the second time. Amanda was arguing that she should be allowed to have the picket, which was now the highest jump in the course, because she was on a horse rather than a pony.

'If you did the picket, you'd have to come all the way over to the east side of the ring and you'd lose time,' Kristen reasoned. 'Don't worry about Dozz clearing 1 metre. She's dealt with 1.30 metres in the Grand Prix.'

'Stop showing off,' Amanda said sulkily. 'The only reason you've got such a fancy pony is 'cause of your mum.'

Jade, who was helping raise the last jump, caught Michaela's eye as they both heard Amanda's comment. Michaela's lips were pursed, as if they were holding in her mouth several words that she knew she shouldn't say.

'Fine,' replied Kristen. 'I'll swap you that nice little, pony-sized yellow oxer for the big horse-sized picket. This means we'll both take way longer than we have to, but it's not a real competition so I don't care.'

'When you've finished bickering, girls, you might like to start the course' Michaela said, ringing the bell.

Dorian and Blueberry Tart, both lean grey show-jumpers, would have looked impressive cantering slowly around the ring if it weren't for their angry riders. Kristen gave little of her mood away, but she was holding Dorian back more than necessary as she went through her start flags. Amanda was doing the same, and Blue, a young thoroughbred, was clearly frustrated.

Once they'd started, the girls rode hard, as if competing against each other rather than together. Instead of pausing to let Kristen go first as they intersected after the second jump, Amanda barged past, leaving Dorian almost crashing into Blue's hindquarters.

Threatened by the sudden proximity of the pony, Blue struck out irritably with her near hindleg. By luck or quick thinking, Kristen pulled Dorian in a hard left-hand turn and saved her pony from a hoof to the breast.

Jade heard Michaela exhale loudly and looked over. The coach's face was frozen and her eyes hard. Although Kristen went clear and Amanda dropped only one rail, when they'd finished Michaela barked, 'You two, over here now!'

Jade hugged Pip's neck and bit her lip as she listened to the older girls getting told off.

'I'm glad that didn't happen to us,' Becca whispered, watching Amanda, who looked like she wanted to cry, riding back to her horse-float. Kristen, who seemed more sullen than upset, set off back to her truck at a gallop.

'Walk the last hundred metres!' Michaela shouted. 'You stupid girl.'

Instead of slowing down, Kristen veered towards the fence line and pointed her pony at a tiger trap that was usually included in the intermediate cross-country course. It was a big, solid obstacle for the

14.2-hand pony, who was used to show-jumps which fell if her hooves touched them. Dorian seemed to hang in mid-air over the log for a long time before landing heavily on the other side.

'Wow!' David said.

'Don't sound so impressed,' Michaela snapped. 'I think it's disgusting how she's venting her anger via Dorian. Never, but never, should you take it out on a horse.'

If David and Corina hadn't completed a fast, clear round during their turn at the Jigsaw, Jade dreaded to think how furious Michaela would have been. But the two eldest team members did a beautiful round, which cooled their coach's temper.

'I wish those naughty girls had seen that,' Michaela said. 'Your round had everything theirs was lacking: co-operation, courtesy, maturity. You've restored my faith in the team. You two littlies did well, too. Let's call it a day on this good note.'

Ordinarily, Jade and Becca would've flinched at being referred to as 'littlies', but that afternoon they were just relieved not to be the ones in Michaela's bad books.

'Just think, only two weeks until the Champs!' Becca said, as the girls prepared their tired ponies for the truck ride home.

'I know! Only one more practice.' Jade grimaced, but really she was more excited than nervous. 'I reckon we'll be ready though.'

'Me, too,' Becca agreed unexpectedly. 'We've improved quite a lot, eh?'

'Yeah, Pip's way fitter now; and the nightly hard feed seems to have given her more energy. If I'm not too nervous on the day, we'll be fine.' Even just mentioning the actual competition made Jade's heart beat a bit faster, though.

'Our team might even win — if only that nasty Amanda can stop herself from sabotaging Kristen's rounds.' Becca said this in her excited outdoor voice, without realizing whose float was parked next to their truck.

'Don't you speak about my daughter like that!' Amanda's mother, who'd been quietly reading a *Cuisine* magazine in the driver's seat, opened the door and stepped out. She was a tall, imposing woman wearing pearls, an Aertex shirt and a sickly perfume.

Becca went pale. 'I'm sorry. I didn't know you were there.'

'Obviously not.'

'I'm sorry,' Becca said again, weakly. 'I only said it because Michaela told Amanda and Kristen off just now.'

'Amanda *and* Kristen? So it wasn't just my daughter's fault?'

'I guess not.'

'I'm glad we've got that straight. I expect you're just jealous of Mandy, but it's no excuse.'

'Why would Rebecca be jealous of Amanda?' Becca's mum cut in, emerging from the cab of the truck.

'No, Mum, don't!' Becca pleaded.

'Load the ponies, girls,' Becca's mum ordered. Jade and Becca did what they were told. From inside the truck they heard the mothers carrying on the argument.

'Mum, we're ready to go,' Becca said quietly, when Amanda's mother had finished ranting about cheap ponies and bad company.

'Right, we're off,' Becca's mum said. As she backed the truck out, Jade saw Amanda, who'd been hiding on the other side of the float with Blue, mouthing 'Sorry!' at them.

'Gosh, you can see where Amanda gets it from, can't you?' Becca's mum said with a forced laugh. 'I'm going to have to stay out of that woman's way if she comes to Cambridge, I think.'

'What did she mean about bad company?' Jade asked.

'Nothing, sweet. She was just being small-minded.'

'Was it about Jade?' Becca asked, shocked.

'Don't worry about it, love,' Becca's mum said.

'Was it because of Jade's dad?' Becca persisted.

'Leave it, Becca!' Becca's mum snapped. She could see that Jade was looking uncomfortable.

'What would I have done without you?' Jade said to Pip as she let her go in the paddock that night. 'You're so much nicer than most people.'

Jade watched her black pony trot down to the back fence to see Brandy and Hamlet. She looked slightly stiff and was raising her head in the air at each stride. *That's odd*, Jade thought, trying to remember if there had been any heat in Pip's legs when she was washing them. No, surely she wasn't lame. It was probably just the low dusk light.

During lunch break the next day at school, Mr White called Jade on her cellphone, something he'd never done before.

'What's going on?' Jade asked, instantly worried.

'Jade, I'm sorry to call you at school like this. You're not in class, are you?'

'No. Is it Pip? What's happened?'

'I just thought I ought to tell you as soon as possible, what with the Champs coming up: Pip's lame.'

Jade's face started to tingle. 'How do you know?'

'Well, she was lying down this morning when I took the horses some hay, which is unusual for her. She didn't even get up when I went over to say hello and she was sweating. Anyway, I got her halter on and pulled her to her feet, but she was obviously in pain, so I walked her slowly back to the yards and called

Dan Lewis straight away.' Dan Lewis, Michaela's husband, was a specialist equine vet.

'Has he been yet?' Jade asked, not even stopping to worry about the cost.

'Yes, I thought I'd wait for his diagnosis before I called you, just in case I'd fussed over nothing.'

'It's not nothing, though, is it?'

'No. It's laminitis, Jade.'

Jade thought back to her C-Certificate study. Equine diseases hadn't really interested her, although she remembered a symptom of laminitis because it had made her and Becca wish they hadn't skipped ahead to the B-Certificate section when she'd read aloud the description. In acute cases, the pedal bone would rotate inside the hoof, sometimes even pushing through the sole.

'I thought only fat ponies got laminitis?' Jade said. 'Pip's never been fitter.'

'I'll tell you all about what Dan said after school,' Mr White replied, trying to soothe Jade. 'I've done my best to make Pip comfortable: she's in the shady yard and has had a small feed of chaff with Bute powder. That's easing the pain for now.'

Jade thanked Mr White and promised she'd be around straight after school.

'I want to go now!' she said, after explaining the situation to Laura and Becca. 'I hate thinking of her in all that pain.'

'Poor Pip!' Laura said, looking almost as devastated as Jade. 'And poor you. All that training down the drain.'

'Yeah, what will happen to the team?' Becca said.

Jade felt sick with disappointment. She and Pip would no longer be going to the Champs.

Dorian the Grey

Pip whinnied to Jade as she saw her friend bike up the driveway.

Mr White was hosing Pip's front hooves, which made Jade feel guilty for not being with her sick pony all afternoon.

'What did the vet say?' Jade asked, taking the hose from Mr White. 'How did this happen? She was fine yesterday.' Well, almost — Jade remembered Pip's stiff gait in the paddock the night before and felt another stab of guilt.

'Acute laminitis can come on suddenly, although even Dan was unsure of what caused it. Possibly all the jumping on hard ground, or maybe the richer feed we were giving Pip each night.'

'So it's my fault?' Jade said, frowning.

'No, not at all!' Mr White replied. 'You've never let Pip get too fat, and you haven't been riding her into the ground. It's just terrible, terrible luck, that's all.'

Jade sniffed loudly. 'What can I do to help her get better?'

'Well,' Mr White looked serious, 'I've already given her as much Bute powder as she's allowed for tonight — that's eased the pain a bit. While she's happy to stand up, you might like to walk her slowly around the paddock for five minutes, just to get the blood circulating in her hooves. The hose water might have soothed the inflammation, but it also slows down the blood flow.'

Jade frowned. She was trying to imagine the inside of Pip's front hooves: the pedal bone in the middle, holding up the pony's weight, and fanning out from the pedal bone, the laminae. In Jade's mind they resembled ropes, running from the wall of the hoof to the pedal bone, taking all the pressure of Pip's weight as she cantered and jumped. The laminitis, like a rat, had gnawed at the laminae ropes. They were now breaking and Pip's poor pedal bone was dangling free from the hoof wall. Instead of having her whole hoof holding her up, the bone was taking all the pressure.

With these images in her head, Jade couldn't see how Pip would ever recover.

'Walking her, hosing her and giving her Bute will only stop the pain,' Jade said, raising her voice. 'How can we make her *better*?'

'Let's just concentrate on keeping her comfortable for now. That'll mean taking her shoes off and making the ground in the yard a bit softer.'

'I'll phone Mr Finch!' Jade said. 'And Granddad might know where to get wood shavings. Though I should call Dad first.'

Jade didn't know exactly how much Dan Lewis would charge for each visit, or how costly the sachets of Bute were, but she had a bad feeling that it was all going to be expensive.

'Look, Jade, why don't you go home and tell your dad about this now. There's nothing more you can do for Pip this evening.'

'I can keep her company!' Jade argued. 'And you

just said it'd help if I walked her around.'

Clipping the lead rope onto Pip's halter, Jade patted her pony's sweaty neck and said, 'C'mon, girl, let's go for a wee walk.'

Pip threw her head up in the air and put her ears back. All the pony's weight was resting on her back legs now and her front hooves were stretched out in front.

'C'mon,' Jade tried again, pulling on the lead rope. Pip gave her a dirty look and nipped at her shoulder.

'She doesn't want to walk,' Jade said to Mr White, hopelessly.

'I know,' Mr White replied. 'It's a very hard thing, coaxing a pony that sore into walking. Abby's friend's pony had laminitis and it was heartbreaking having to chase such a sick pony with a whip to make it move.'

'Why do it?' Jade asked. 'Wouldn't walking just make it worse?'

'Maybe,' Mr White said. 'Some people think it's cruel; others think that blood circulation is a necessary part of the cure. Dan suggested walking Pip, so that's why I said you should try it.'

Firmly stroking Pip's neck, Jade willed her pony to trust her and try walking a few steps. Chatting nonsensically to distract Pip from the pain, Jade eventually cajoled her into taking three agonizing steps. Seeing the pony that had cleared a 90-centimetre course just the day before struggling to even walk made Jade want to cry. She couldn't stop herself — the tears just started spilling out.

'Are we allowed to feed her anything, as a treat?' Jade asked Mr White, after she'd wiped her eyes.

'I've been giving her little feeds of chaff with the Bute mixed in. Rich grass and grain feed, like we've been feeding her, is a no-no though.'

'What about a carrot or apple?'

'I don't see why not.'

'I'll bring some tomorrow then,' Jade said, sniffing again. 'Thanks very much for looking after her today.'

'What else was I going to do?' Mr White said, laughing weakly.

When Jade got home, her granddad was sitting on the

deck with her dad, reading the paper and swigging a beer. Dumping her school bag on her bed, Jade poured herself a glass of juice and joined them.

'Granddad,' she asked, 'do you know where I could get some wood shavings?'

Without looking up from the paper, he replied, 'Murray Burgess has a joinery just out of Flaxton. He might have some shavings.'

'I knew you'd know someone,' Jade said, cheering up slightly.

'Is this for Pip?' her dad asked, noticing Jade's puffy eyes.

'Pip's really sick, Dad,' Jade said, her voice wobbling.

As she described the sorry state of her pony, her dad put an arm around her and listened intently.

'I think it's going to cost heaps,' Jade said.

'Don't worry about that, love,' her dad said seriously. 'Pip's part of our family now, and we'll all do our best to help her get well. Oh, you poor old soul,' he said, rubbing Jade's back as she was struck by another bout of sobbing.

'I've just given Murray a call,' Granddad said, emerging from the kitchen. 'I can pick up a couple of bags of shavings tomorrow and take them around to the invalid.'

'You're awesome, Granddad!' Jade said. 'That reminds me, Dad, we need to call Mr Finch. Pip will be more comfortable with her shoes off.'

It was an evening of phone calls. After Jade had arranged for the farrier to visit the next afternoon at four, Jade's dad called Mr White. He made sure that Jade was distracted by her dinner and the TV before asking directly how good Pip's chances were for a recovery.

'We'll know how bad it is once the X-rays are back,' Mr White said gravely. 'The vet said he'd be in touch tomorrow afternoon.'

'Right; well, fingers crossed then. I really appreciate your help with this, Jim. Make sure you forward all the bills to me.'

'Will do. I think you should prepare Jade for the worst, though. It's likely that Pip will never be ridden again, and that the kindest thing may be to put her down.'

The last phone call of the evening was to Michaela.

'Oh, Jade, Dan told me the sad news,' Michaela said. 'And Pip was going so well, too.'

'I know,' Jade said in a small voice. 'Sorry for letting the team down.'

'It's not your fault!' Michaela replied. 'But it has thrown a spanner in the works. Don't worry, though, I'll think of something.'

'Now I'm officially out of the team,' Jade said calmly, hanging up the phone. 'I guess we'll just have to try again next year.'

Jade's dad muted the TV. 'Love, you know that there's a good chance Pip won't recover from this?'

Jade knew very well, but hated hearing her dad say it. 'How would you know? You don't know anything about horses!' she shouted.

'I talked to Mr White, Jade.'

'You just want to get Pip put down so you don't have to pay vet bills!' Jade hissed in a poisonous voice.

'Jade, I know you're upset, but please don't be horrible,' her dad implored. 'I just want you to be prepared for the worst. I hope the worst won't come, but if it does I want you to be ready.'

Pip was the reason Jade had wanted to stay in Flaxton. Pip had helped Jade through a very hard year. Jade felt like she'd never be ready for Pip's death, and she certainly didn't want to talk about it with her dad right then, in the kitchen, with the smell of spaghetti bolognaise still hanging in the air. Jade ran to her bedroom and slammed the door.

The next afternoon, Jade's granddad picked her up from school and drove her straight to Mr White's. The back of the big white Falcon was filled with bags of wood shavings. While her granddad drove, Jade wondered what the vet would have to say about Pip's X-ray.

When they pulled into the driveway, Mr White and the farrier were in the yard with Pip, one standing at her head, comforting her, while the other cut the clenches and pulled her front shoes off.

'I daren't take off the back ones today,' Mr Finch said, wiping his brow with his forearm. 'She's much too sore to hold herself up on her front hooves right now. Anyway, the hind shoes have got another month's wear in them at least, and they're not bothering her.'

Jade thanked the farrier for coming around at such short notice. As he was leaving the Whites', his ute nearly collided with the Lewises' four-wheel-drive.

'Rush hour at the Whites',' Dan said pleasantly, as he hopped out of the driver's seat with a large envelope. 'Before we all look at the X-ray,' he said, 'how's the patient? Did the Bute help, Jim?' Dan went over to Pip and let her rest her forehead against his shoulder. She seemed to understand that he was trying to help her.

'She doesn't look any better,' Mr White replied. 'But no worse either, so that's something.'

'This is good,' Dan said, motioning at the wood shavings that Jade was spreading as evenly as she could over the yard. 'Pip will probably be tempted to lie down more often now she's got a comfy bed, but you don't want her to get sores, or lose circulation, so remember to walk her.'

Jade looked dismayed. 'I know it's hard,' Dan went on, seeing her face, 'but it's good for her.'

'Is there any point in making her walk if she's

just going to be put down eventually?' Jade said, surprising everyone.

'Let's not get ahead of ourselves,' Dan said. 'Have a look at this X-ray with me, and I'll show you why I think we have reason to be optimistic.'

Granddad, Mr White and Jade all peered over the vet's shoulder as he pointed at the blurry white shape in the middle of the hoof's outline.

'This is the pedal bone. It should be sitting at this angle.' The vet drew a line with his finger. 'But because the laminae have frayed, it's started rotating. But,' he said triumphantly, 'and this is the important detail, it hasn't rotated completely. If it had, you might see the bone poking through the skin and the hoof dangling like a mitten.'

Jade flinched.

'If that were the case,' Dan continued, 'I'd suggest putting Pip down. It'd be cruel to keep her in that state. But, as she is, I think we should give her a good chance to recover.' He looked serious for a moment. 'When I say "recover", Jade, I mean to paddock fitness. Pip will never jump again.'

'That's OK,' Jade said, unconvincingly.

'When you think that she's nearly twenty-four,' Mr White said, patting Jade on the shoulder, 'retirement doesn't seem like such a bad option.'

'And,' Dan added, 'I've known some ponies who had laminitis who recovered enough to make good beginners' mounts. I can't make any promises that Pip will recover to that degree, but it's something to keep in mind while you're nursing her.'

Jade nodded and stroked her pony's nose. 'We'll help you get better, girl. Don't worry.'

After the tiring excitement of visitors, Pip painfully eased herself to the ground and lay on the new bedding with her front legs tucked up like a dog's. Jade sat down next to her pony and rested her back against Pip's shoulder. When Pip was well, Jade would never have done this, for fear that she'd get trodden on. But, right now, Pip wasn't going anywhere in a hurry and she seemed to enjoy Jade's quiet company.

Jade and her granddad arrived home to a dark house. Her dad was working late. There was a note on the bench saying, 'Don't worry about dinner: I'll bring home pizza', and a red light flashing on the answerphone.

The new message was from Michaela, asking Jade to call her immediately. With her school bag still hanging on her shoulder, Jade quickly dialled the number.

'Jade, it's good to hear from you,' Michaela said quickly, answering after the first ring. 'Kristen and I have been talking about the team, and we have a proposition for you.'

'OK,' Jade replied, wondering whether they'd decided to let her come along as a groom. 'Have you found someone new already?'

'No, Jade,' Michaela said. 'At this late stage we'd rather you stayed on the team. Would you be willing to ride Kristen's pony, Dorian?'

The lean grey had soared over a 1.30-metre oxer in the pony Grand Prix last season, and as Jade had watched she'd wished that she was her rider.

'What about Kristen?' Jade asked, confused.

'Kristen has a young pony, Johnny, that she's been bringing on. He's had a couple of outings and has behaved sensibly, so I don't see why she couldn't compete on him at the Champs,' Michaela said. 'In fact, I don't know why we didn't consider it sooner. It'll be a great chance for prospective buyers to see him in action. So, you're keen? Dorian's a pro; she'll show you a good time.'

'Yeah, of course! Thank you so much,' Jade babbled. 'But is pony-swapping allowed?'

'It's not encouraged,' Michaela said, 'but I've been on the phone to the organizers and explained our unfortunate situation. I convinced them in the end and our entry has been changed.'

In between mouthfuls of pizza, Jade told her dad and granddad the news. She'd promised to go round to the Lewises' straight after school the next day, for a practice.

'What about Pip?' her granddad asked. 'I thought you were going to nurse her each day after school. That's what you told the vet.'

'I'll go in the morning, before school. And Mr White can give her Bute in the afternoon.'

'Pip's your pony, not Jim White's,' her granddad grumbled. 'You shouldn't take him for granted.'

'I'm not!' Jade said. 'It's just I can't be everywhere at once!'

'Dad, leave her alone,' Jade's father said to Granddad.

'I don't want her neglecting her old sick pony as soon as she's offered a fancy new one,' Granddad said. 'That's all.'

'Jade won't neglect Pip. I know she won't. Perhaps, Jade,' her dad suggested, 'while you're busy riding this new pony, you could ask for some help from Laura and Becca? They want to be vets, don't they?'

'Laura does, but only small animals,' Jade replied sadly. 'And Granddad's right: I shouldn't neglect Pip.'

'You shouldn't let your team down either,' her dad said. 'How about I bike around and see to Pip tomorrow after work? You'll have to write me a list of what to do, though.'

Feeling ridiculous biking in her riding helmet and jodhpurs on the way to the Lewises', Jade wondered how her dad would get on with the list. She'd asked him to muck out the yard, put down fresh shavings, mix a small feed with a sachet of Bute, hose Pip's hooves and coax her to take a few steps. For someone unaccustomed to horses, this would be quite a challenge. Jade hoped that her dad would manage.

In the Lewises' own pristine yards, Kristen was grooming Dorian.

'I would've groomed her,' Jade said, propping her bike against the fence. 'It's the least I could do. Thanks so much for lending her to me.'

'You haven't ridden her yet,' Kristen said in an ominous voice. 'You might want to save your thanks.'

Jade looked nervous.

'Nah, just kidding. She's a sweetheart when you're on her back. Mean when you're on the ground, though,' Kristen admitted, dodging a nip as she brushed under Dorian's stomach. 'See? That's why I didn't leave her for you to groom.'

Kristen was right. As soon as Jade mounted Dorian, she could tell she was on a well-schooled pony. Dorian was as sensible and honest as Pip, but also as nimble and energetic as Dusty. It took only very light aids to get her to change pace and her ears were always twitching, listening intelligently.

'I think she knows more than I do,' Jade said, sitting deeper in the expensive black jumping saddle.

'Quite possibly,' Michaela said. 'She's a smart cookie, that one.'

Also in need of last-minute training, Kristen and Jack Sparrow, a fine-featured dark bay gelding affectionately known as Johnny, followed Jade and Dorian around the practice ring. At Michaela's command, the girls walked, trotted and cantered their mounts on each rein.

'Dorian's looking good, Jade, but she has a tendency to fall in on the left rein. Watch out for that — keep her balanced and interested. Don't let her fall asleep.'

There was no chance of that when they started trying out the practice course. After Jade had taken her over a 90-centimetre straight-bar, Dorian threw a playful buck. Jade could hear Kristen laughing.

'You know what it is?' Kristen told Jade as they both slowed back down to a trot. 'You're a fair bit lighter than me, and I'm pretty much the only one who's ridden her in the last three or four years. She's probably enjoying the weight off her back.'

The buck had shaken Jade. She'd started to take it for granted that Dorian was a push-button pony that would do no wrong. Now she was more cautious. Trying a course of five jumps this time, Jade rode more actively. Dorian often needed no help in finding the right stride, but that didn't mean that Jade should just be a passenger. She started asking more of Dorian — cutting corners, approaching jumps on an angle — and the grey mare responded well. When Michaela suggested they call it a day, Jade felt like she and Dorian were beginning to forge a mutual respect.

'Phew! I think the team might be OK after all,' Michaela said, letting out a sigh.

'You never doubted us, did you?' Kristen laughed.

'Oh, I don't know; it felt like the team was cursed for a moment there, what with Pip's bad luck,' Michaela said, taking the saddle from Jade, who was unsure of where to put it. The Lewises didn't have just a dusty implement shed, but a proper stable with a tack room. Everything looked as clean and ordered as Mrs White's kitchen; Jade was scared to ruin it.

'Dad told me about poor Pip,' Kristen said, once Dorian and Johnny had been given their feeds.

'She'll be OK,' Jade said uncertainly. 'I mean, she's not good now; she can barely stand up. But your dad reckons she has an OK chance of recovering.'

'It's very hard losing a pony,' Michaela said. 'I've been there and so has Kristen. Remember Foxy, Kris?' Kristen nodded briefly, but didn't look up. 'The point is that you'll need to spend lots of time with Pip, especially as you'll be going to Cambridge for three days in a week-and-a-half.'

'Is it only a week-and-a-half away?' Kristen asked, shocked.

'That's right. It's crept up on us. Ideally, I'd have you practising every day, getting really familiar with Dorian, but I understand if that isn't possible.'

'It might be,' Kristen said. 'What if Dozz stayed at Mr White's for the next week? I'd miss her, but it'd be a good way for Jade and her to bond. And I know Jade would take good care of her.'

Michaela thought about this. 'That's not a bad idea at all. Do you think Mr White would mind, Jade?'

Jade didn't see why he would. Now that Pip was confined to the yard, there was an extra paddock free.

'Well, in that case,' Michaela said decisively, 'I'll bring her round tomorrow afternoon. You'll be there, I take it?'

Jade nodded, hoping that Mr White wouldn't mind, and, more importantly, that Pip wouldn't mind. Jade didn't want her sick pony to feel like she'd been replaced.

Butterflies

'OK, I think we've remembered everything,' Kristen said, unpacking the last of Dorian's pristine gear from the truck. The pony herself had just been let loose in Mr White's front paddock, and, not bothering to say hello to Brandy and Hamlet down the back, had immediately started grazing. Pip had pricked her ears and whinnied at the familiar face, but had not moved from the corner of her yard.

'Thanks,' Jade said, uncomfortably aware that Kristen's valuable possessions were her responsibility for the next week.

'If anything happens, don't be afraid to call,' Michaela said.

Kristen saw Jade's worried face. 'I'm sure you'll be fine. Dozz is so chilled out, she already seems at home here.'

Dorian was now standing next to Pip's yard, sniffing at the sick pony's nose.

'Leave her alone, Dorian!' Michaela called. 'She's an invalid.'

'I think she likes the new company,' Jade said.

'Poor old thing looks so sore,' Kristen said. 'You probably won't want to leave her next week, eh?'

Jade shook her head. But a small part of her was actually glad to be getting away. It was gruelling seeing Pip's pain every day and not being able to do much about it.

'That reminds me,' Michaela said. 'I've got a list of things you'll need in Cambridge.' She rifled around in the cab of the truck, then passed Jade a piece of paper. 'Be here, ready, with all the items on the list, at seven next Friday morning. We'll be picking up Amanda after you, so don't be late.'

Jade promised to be ready on time, and waved as the Lewises' huge truck drove out the Whites' front gate, taking a branch off one of the beech trees with it.

Not wanting to waste the last hours of daylight, Jade put Dorian in the yard next to Pip's, groomed her briefly — having always worn a cover or summer sheet, the grey pony's coat was in excellent condition — and tacked up for a quick ride.

Mr and Mrs White were out, so Jade, for once heeding the adults' warning, concentrated on flat work. The jumps were tempting, but on a new pony, and without anyone to call the ambulance if she fell off, Jade cautiously avoided them. Instead she acquainted herself with Dorian's gait and noticed that, although obviously well-schooled, even she had a few faults. At the trot, she had a tendency to over-bend — the opposite of Pip, who was often reluctant to stay on the bit.

After twenty minutes of walking, trotting and cantering on each rein — the highlight of which was discovering Dorian's talent for flying changes, some-thing Jade had never quite mastered with Pip — Jade rewarded the obedient pony with a cross-country canter around the long side paddock.

Shortening her stirrups two notches, Jade once again admired Kristen's stunning saddle. Jade made up her mind to give it a thorough clean at least once before Saturday. *This will be a busy week,* Jade thought grimly, as she and Dorian flew around the paddock. The wind was in her face, and there was that comforting smell of wet grass after the much-needed shower earlier that afternoon.

Jade tried to relax and enjoy herself, but in her head she was organizing the next few days. She'd have to be up by six each morning if she was going to have time to shower, breakfast, nurse Pip, muck out the paddock and finish her homework, all before class. *Never mind,* Jade thought philosophically. *I shouldn't complain — it could be worse.* Pip's laminitis could be fatal rather than gradually (as they all hoped) improving. Kristen could have decided not to lend Dorian to Jade, which would have meant not going to the Champs. Worse still, Jade's dad could have made her move back to Auckland at the start of the year, stopping her from riding altogether. If there hadn't been the car accident — if Jade's mum hadn't died — none of this busy week would be happening.

Shocked at how her mind ran away with her during

cross-country canters, Jade brought Dorian back to a trot, then a walk, patting the handsome neck, sleek, silver and muscular as a dolphin.

'It's good to be busy,' Jade told the pony as they walked on a loose rein back to the yards. 'I'm lucky to have you. And thanks for being friendly to Pip. She likes having you here.'

Jade thought this again later as she sat on the top rail of the fence, watching the two mares contentedly eating their feeds. She didn't rest for long, though; the paddock needed mucking out and if she didn't start now, she wouldn't be home in time for dinner.

'Are you keeping up at school?' her dad asked, concerned as Jade yawned between mouthfuls of chicken salad.

'Yeah,' Jade sighed, not looking up from her plate.

'I'm not nagging,' her dad replied. 'It's just that you seem exhausted from all the time you've been spending with the ponies. And you hardly ever mention school any more. I've missed hearing about Mr Wilde's antics.'

'I am keeping up; it's fine,' Jade said, putting down her knife and fork. 'Mr Wilde would probably tell you if I was getting behind. And he wouldn't be so good about me having Friday off, although he does want to see a note from you.'

'Fair enough, that sounds OK. Remind me to write that note straight after dinner, otherwise I'll forget.'

'You won't forget to visit Pip, will you?' Jade asked.

'Perish the thought!' her dad said, in mock offence. 'Between Mr White, your granddad and myself, that pony will have around-the-clock care. I do wish I could come and watch you in action at the Champs, though.'

On Thursday evening, Jade's dad fussed almost as much as her mother would have.

'You can't take that sleeping bag: the zip's broken!' he exclaimed, holding Michaela's list in one hand and a pen in the other. 'What would the pony club mums think of me if I sent you to the Championships with a broken sleeping bag?'

'Relax, Dad,' Jade said. 'All that matters is that my

boots are polished, my shirt's ironed, and my tie, jersey and jodhpurs are clean.'

'Are they?'

'Yes, sir!' Jade saluted.

'Excellent. And you've packed a handkerchief?'

Jade rolled her eyes. 'Dad! I don't even have a cold.'

'What about your badge? You're always losing that.'

'Not this time!' Jade grinned. The little gold and blue oval, with a horse's head inside a horseshoe and a tiny 'C' at the bottom, that Jade had earned when she passed her C-certificate exam, was safely zipped inside her sponge bag.

Finally, with her jeans and T-shirt laid out for the next morning, and her alarm set for a quarter to six, Jade fell into bed, exhausted. But she couldn't stop worrying about the next few days. There were already butterflies in her stomach, just thinking about the competition.

'Dad, I can't sleep!' Jade called through the wall.

'Try reading a chapter of *Oliver Twist*,' her dad called back. 'You told me that was boring you to tears.'

Although her dad's suggestion had been in jest, the plan worked. After only two pages, Jade was fast asleep, with the book on her face. Quietly her dad put *Oliver Twist* on the floor, turned off the bedside lamp and kissed her forehead. He was worried, too, but more about the long drive to Cambridge than the showjumping.

When the Lewises' truck arrived at the Whites', on the dot of seven, Jade, Dorian and their pile of belongings were all ready to go.

'She looks very professional,' Jade's dad said, admiring Dorian as Jade threw on her immaculate travel sheet, first crossing the back straps, then buckling the front.

'Has she been good for you this week?' Michaela asked, taking the pony from Jade and leading her up the ramp of the truck. The reunion of the paddock mates, Johnny and Dorian, involved much whinnying, which set Pip off.

'Poor old lady; you have to stay here,' Jade apologized, giving her pony one last hug. 'I promise I'll be back in a few days. And you'll be well looked after.'

'You certainly will,' said Mr White, who'd come out to say goodbye. 'No need to worry about her, Jade. You have fun and bring back some nice big ribbons.'

'Take care, love,' her dad said, squeezing her shoulder, not wanting to embarrass her in front of her friends. 'I'll have my fingers crossed for you on Saturday and Sunday.'

'I'll look after her like she's my own,' Michaela told Jade's dad with a wink.

Hearing Pip's frantic neighing and watching her dad and Mr White waving at the fence, Jade's throat tightened.

'Gosh, Pip misses you already,' Kristen said. 'Dorian didn't seem to notice at all when I left her with you last week.'

'Actually, I think it's Dorian that Pip misses,' Jade said, smiling. 'They've become surprisingly good friends.'

Amanda's house was down a narrow driveway lined with cyprus trees.

'I'll never get the truck through,' Michaela decided

finally, stopping at the gateway. 'Could you two go in and tell Amanda I'm parked out here?'

'That's ludicrous! No one's ever had trouble with the driveway before,' Amanda's mother said when Kristen explained the situation.

They made a slow procession to the truck with Amanda at the front, leading an excitable Blueberry Tart, Kristen next, carrying tack and grooming tools, Jade third, with the buckets and feed, and finally Mrs Nisbet in the rear, lugging Amanda's suitcase.

'Don't let the team down,' Mrs Nisbet said sternly to Amanda, once the horse was loaded and the gear stowed. Mother and daughter pecked each other on the cheek briefly, and then they were away.

Being on the road seemed a relief to everyone. Amanda, who wasn't a morning person, soon fell asleep. The rest of them played Horse for the next twenty minutes or so, a simple game in which the player who spots the most horses wins (foals were worth two points and donkeys three). The game had to be abandoned once they'd passed the Shetland pony farm, though; as everyone lost count, and it was difficult to tell which ones were the foals.

'I think I got thirty-five points,' Kristen said competitively.

'OK, looks like you won then,' her mother replied. 'Hey, Jade, have you heard from Becca this morning? Maybe you could send her a text while we've got reception and see whether they're running to schedule. I was hoping we might have lunch with them in Turangi.'

'They should be ahead of us,' Jade said. She'd received three texts from Becca already this morning, mostly complaining about not knowing what to say to Corina and David, who seemed pretty much grown-up at seventeen. Becca's mum, as formidably efficient as Michaela, had ensured that her cargo was safely boarded by seven-thirty.

'No problems, then? Everyone present?'

'I think Medusa was tough to load, but other than that, no.'

'Chestnut mares, eh? Pigs, the lot of them; except my mum's little hunter, Angel. She was sweet as they come — the first horse I rode.'

Jade, who'd heard a little about Michaela's horsey history when she'd done a school project on the Olympian last year, was eager to hear more.

'Did you show-jump Angel?' Jade asked.

'For one season. She wasn't clever enough or big enough to go to the top, though. Her real forte was on the hunting field. She was sensible but with plenty of stamina, and manners; what some people would call a "lady's hunter".'

For the next 30 kilometres, the four riders debated whether there was such a thing as a 'girl's pony' or a 'boy's pony'. Even Amanda, who'd just woken up from her nap, joined in, saying that she thought such distinctions were rubbish. Jade used the case of Floyd as an example of a horse that preferred males.

'That's different, though, isn't it?' Kristen said. 'If Lisa had been a man, Floyd would've been put off men. It was her fault.'

'Probably,' Michaela said. 'But who really knows? I don't know if horses judge their riders based on gender, but I've definitely seen certain horse-and-rider combinations that have really clicked.'

'Like human relationships,' Amanda said.

'To some extent, but not exactly,' Michaela went on. 'It doesn't help to personify horses, to forget that they're not the same species as us. In that sense, the relationship between horse and rider is more impressive. At its best, it involves immense trust, loyalty and respect.'

'Isn't that Becca's truck?' Kristen said, leaning across Amanda and staring out the window. 'Mum, stop!'

Remembering the horses in the back, Michaela indicated, slowed gradually and pulled over onto the grass verge.

'Yeah, it's Becca,' Jade said, worried.

'Kristen and Amanda, you stay here and supervise our lot. Refill the hay-nets if need be. Jade, you can come with me and see what's happened.'

The grass verge was sufficiently wide for a parked truck, but the busy road made it a less than ideal spot for unloading horses.

'Morning,' Michaela said calmly to Becca's mum, who looked frazzled. She and David were lowering the truck's ramp. 'What's happened?'

'Medusa's gone down,' David said. 'Corina and

161

Becca are inside. They've tried to get her up, but she won't budge. We'll have to unload the others.'

The ramp lowered at the side, rather than the back end, of the truck. Dusty, who'd been loaded first, just to the left of the door, was the easiest to get out. Panicked and sweaty, he didn't wait for Becca to untie his lead rope, but pulled back violently, snapping the loop of twine to which he'd been tied and scraping his rump on the truck's side as he careered out backwards.

'Easy does it; steady, boy,' Michaela said, still sounding implausibly calm.

Jade's job was to keep an eye out for cars, and as far as was possible signal to them to slow down. 'Clear!' Jade shouted, fortunately just as Dusty came shooting out backwards onto the road.

'You stupid girl!' Becca's mum scolded her daughter. 'I told you to untie his lead rope and hang it over his neck before we put the ramp down. That way you could've kept a hold on him instead of letting him run out into the traffic. He could've been killed!'

Becca couldn't help it; she started crying. 'No harm done,' Michaela said gently. 'That's the main thing.'

Becca's mum, embarrassed at her outburst, took

Dusty's lead rope and tried to calm him down behind the truck. Becca followed, wanting to soothe her frightened pony.

David's horse, Toby, was keen to disembark, too. But, unlike the skittish pony, he was sensibly cautious of the traffic and had to be helped out by his rider.

'Wait!' Jade shouted, as a blue SUV sped around the corner. Jade flinched, hating its driver for a moment. Didn't he know how dangerous he was being? 'Clear!' she called, watching the vehicle disappear around the next corner.

With Toblerone safely out and standing, shivering, next to a slightly calmer Dusty, Medusa was now visible in the back. She was a dark shape, showing the whites of her eyes and struggling. Corina was at her head, stroking her neck and tugging on the halter as best she could. 'Get up, you silly goose!' Corina growled. 'Up you get, silly!' Jade was amazed at Corina's grit. If it had been Pip stuck on her side in a horse-truck, rump sliding about in her own droppings, Jade would've been devastated.

With a sudden lunge of co-operation, Medusa pushed up painfully, front legs stretched out bearing the brunt of her weight until her near-hind hoof had a grip on the twisted rubber mat. A second great heave and a furious snort of pain got the tired mare up on three feet. The off-hind, however, was stuck fast in the wooden panel of the truck.

'Oh no!' Corina exclaimed. 'Michaela, she's kicked through the wall.'

Michaela swore under her breath and went up the ramp to have a look. 'Try and keep her still, Corina,' she instructed. 'I know it's hard.'

The mare, now she was up and could see the open door, was desperate to be out of the truck and with the other horses, out of harm's way. The hot pain in her off-hind fetlock would, in Medusa's mind, stop once she was out of the truck and on the grassy verge. But every time she pushed towards the fresh air, her rider's sharp shoulder was in her chest and her arm was around her neck.

'Do you have an axe or something sharp for cutting out a bit of the wall?' Jade, sent by Michaela, asked Becca's mum. They had a look in the truck's toolkit, but found nothing suitable for the job.

'I always think I'm prepared for everything, then

something like this happens,' Michaela muttered to herself. 'We'll just have to wave a car down, see if someone can help.'

The first car Jade pulled up was a silver Honda Accord, belonging to a young mother who was interested in the horses, but who could offer no axe or saw.

'Hey! That's an AA van,' David shouted to Jade. 'Flag him down.'

Standing as close to the road as she dared, waving and jumping around like an unco-ordinated cheerleader, Jade convinced the driver to stop.

'Would you be able to lend us an axe, please?' she asked, as he opened the driver's door. 'One of our horses has kicked through the side of the truck.'

'Ouch!' he said. 'Let's have a look.'

Taking what felt like forever, the man, who was somewhere between Jade's dad's and granddad's ages, fossicked about in the back of his truck. 'What are we cutting through?' he asked. 'Plywood, I think,' Jade said uncertainly.

The man grinned. 'This should do. Where's the problem?'

Jade took him into the truck, to where Michaela was holding Medusa's off-hind leg to try to stop it kicking.

'Our knight in shining armour,' Michaela said as the AA man knelt beside her and examined the problem.

'Might have to take a fair bit of the wall out,' he apologized. 'And the horse won't like the banging.'

'She got herself into this mess, so she can damn well put up with it,' Michaela said, smiling stiffly. Corina looked pale and tired.

'I've never done this before,' the man said cheerfully, as he started hacking at the wooden wall, dangerously close to Medusa's leg. 'Never thought, when I woke up this morning, that I'd be doing this.'

'Hmm,' Jade said quietly, not wanting to appear rude, but, like everyone else both inside and outside the truck, willing him to work quickly.

'Nearly there,' he said, sweat gathering around his temples as he hacked cautiously around the bottom of the hoof.

'Hear that, bub? You're nearly free,' Corina said in a high voice.

'Give her a pull now, Corina; he's finished,'

Michaela said. 'Let's get her out of here.'

Corina, holding the lead rope with white knuckles, led Medusa towards the truck door. The mare's muscles were stiff and her nerves shattered, but left with no real option but to trust her friend, she pulled with her bad leg. Feeling it come free from the wall, with a rasp of wood and metal, she charged down the ramp; she was wearing an untidy ring of wood like an anklet around her off-hind fetlock, below the travel bandage that had ridden up to her hock.

Michaela let out a long sigh. 'We can't thank you enough for your help. I'm so sorry, I didn't even ask your name?'

'You were distracted. Roger,' the AA man said. 'My pleasure to lend a hand to some damsels, and horses, in distress.'

Michaela tried to give Roger twenty dollars for his time, but he wouldn't hear of it. 'I hope the rest of your trip isn't so dramatic,' he said, giving a quick toot as he drove off.

'What an idiot!' Corina exclaimed. 'Tooting while there are stressed-out horses on the side of the road.'

'Your stressed-out horse wouldn't be on the side

of the road if it weren't for him,' David reminded her. 'She'd still be stuck in the wall of the truck.'

With a couple of angry stamps, Medusa's wounded fetlock was free of its wooden anklet.

'It doesn't look too deep,' Michaela said, sprinkling white disinfectant powder over the cuts, then deftly rolling a bandage around the fetlock. 'I can't see if there are any splinters still stuck in there. We'll unload them all at Turangi and I'll have another look then. This really isn't a good place to linger.'

While the others held the horses, Jade and Becca swiftly refilled the hay-nets, scraped the droppings off the rubber mats and chained off the far end of the truck, where there was now a gaping hole in the wooden wall, showing the dented metal of the truck's exterior.

'Mum's not going to be happy about this,' Becca whispered to Jade.

'At least it happened right at the back. Why wasn't Medusa tied up next to Toby?'

'They kept niggling at each other. Then she kicked him, so we moved her. Do you think we'll ever make it to Cambridge?'

'Of course,' Jade said firmly. 'Medusa will be tired and careful now. She shouldn't make any more trouble.' This was really just wishful thinking, but saying it made Jade feel a bit better.

It was eleven o'clock by the time they set off again, this time with Dusty in between Toblerone and Medusa.

'Will Medusa be fit to jump tomorrow?' Kristen asked, after she and Amanda, who'd only managed to glimpse the action from the Lewises' truck, were brought up to date.

'That's the question,' Michaela said wearily. 'The cuts looked shallow to me, but until we trot her out, it's hard to say. How were our three during the drama?'

'Like sleepy lambs,' Kristen said. 'Dozz was dozing, Blue wouldn't stop eating and Johnny just wanted cuddles.'

Lunchtime came long before the convoy reached Turangi. Not wanting to upset the now peaceful animals, Becca's mum and Michaela allowed for only a five-minute toilet stop and trip to the bakery in Taihape. Peeling a five-dollar note off the small wad of food money her dad had given her the night before, Jade bought a chicken roll and a chocolate lamington. She was concerned that she'd chosen a babyish treat, but got it anyway, not caring what Amanda thought. To Jade's relief, she saw that Kristen had bought a lamington too, and Amanda a custard square.

'Poor Blue,' Amanda laughed, with white icing on her nose, as they drove off again. 'I'll weigh a ton tomorrow.'

'Nonsense,' Michaela said sternly. 'It'll give you the energy you need for a long day's riding.'

'That's not what Mum says,' Amanda replied. 'She's always going on about how I won't get into my jodhpurs if I eat too much junk food.'

'That's horrible!' Kristen said. 'My mum can be pretty mean, but not like that,' she added, earning an elbow in the ribs from Michaela.

At Turangi, there was a toilet stop for both horses and riders. In a large, empty car park off the road, there was plenty of room to let the animals stretch their legs.

Although it was pleasant with a cool breeze coming off the lake, it was already late afternoon and there was no time to enjoy the view. 'I told Mr Parry we'd be there before dark. That won't be happening now,' Michaela fussed.

It was, in fact, nine o'clock as the trucks drove down the Parrys' long driveway. A paddock with four young horses, clearly destined for a racetrack, was to the left and an empty paddock, for the Flaxton team, on the right.

'I love Cambridge,' Kristen said. 'The grass is always so green here, and everyone seems to have nice fences and foals in their paddocks.'

'You have nice fences!' Jade objected.

Michaela laughed. 'Thanks, Jade. And, Kristen, you've only been to racing stables and the showgrounds here; Cambridge isn't all like that.'

The horses, exhausted from their long, stressful journey, were the tired riders' first priority. While Michaela greeted Mr Parry, a semi-retired racehorse breeder, Becca's mum sorted out the humans' sleeping quarters and the team members looked after their own respective mounts.

After half an hour, the horses, relieved to be back in a paddock, were rugged up and contentedly gobbling their dinner. Dorian, whom Jade watched protectively, seemed the least bothered by her new surroundings. Methodically, she kicked at her bucket to move the clumps of feed to where her nose could reach them.

'I feel sick,' Becca said. Dusty was tied to the fence next to Dorian, just out of reach of her bucket. 'I don't know if it's butterflies about tomorrow, or the burger I ate for dinner.'

'You're probably just really tired,' Jade said. 'I know I am. We'll sleep well tonight and be fresh for tomorrow.' Although she wasn't completely sure of this, Jade felt an obligation to console her nervous friend.

'Right, kids,' Becca's mum called. 'Your sleeping bags are unrolled in the sleep-out.' They all flinched at being called kids. 'As soon as those ponies have finished eating, unclip their halters and come inside. We have to be up at five-thirty tomorrow!'

The Showgrounds

Jade woke early; her team-mates were still dark, sleeping shapes around her. She and Becca, being the youngest and apparently the most resilient, had lilos on the floor. Kristen and Michaela were on the bunk beds next to the window, which was beginning to glow greyish-yellow. Amanda and Corina were on the other bunks opposite, both facing the wall, and Corina was snoring gently.

Becca's mum, who'd just got up and was using the shower before the rush that would occur in the next half-hour, had the single bed near the door. She'd offered this to David, claiming to be just as comfortable on the mattress in her truck, but he'd declined. *Poor David*, Jade thought, resting her eyes for another five minutes before getting up. *He really is outnumbered.* Wondering whether, out in the truck, he was beginning to wake up, Jade took a deep breath, threw off her sleeping bag and stood up in the chilly air. After a long, hot summer, Jade had almost forgotten the discomfort of a cold morning.

'Good girl, getting up so early,' Becca's mum whispered, coming out of the steamy en suite with her hair in a towel turban. 'Help yourself to the shower. It has good pressure but I reckon that by the time we've all used it the hot water will have run out.'

After a quick, scalding-hot shower, Jade felt much more ready to face the day. While the others were having a bleary eyed discussion about who would have the next shower, Jade followed Becca's mum into Mr Parry's house to help organize breakfast.

Mr Parry was already up, listening to 'Country Life' on National Radio and sipping coffee. The dining room, kitchen and living area were open plan, and every surface seemed to be decorated with racing paraphernalia: the mantelpieces held silver cups and bronze statues of horses; every wall had framed photographs or paintings of thoroughbreds; clippings from the racing section of the newspaper were held to the fridge door with magnets — and even the magnets were horsey, advertising horse dentists and feed suppliers.

'I was about to come out and wake all you girls up myself,' Mr Parry said, chortling hoarsely. 'It's nearly half-past-six.'

Jade smiled nervously and looked at Becca's mum. 'Thanks so much for letting us stay, Mr Parry,' Becca's mum said. 'I'm Christine, and this is Jade, our youngest team member. I've just got to fetch our box of food from the truck; Jade can tell you all about our dramas on the road yesterday.'

Wishing she could have fetched the box instead of being left to make conversation, Jade reluctantly described Medusa's fall.

Mr Parry looked unimpressed when she'd finished, as if a hoof through the wall of the truck was nothing compared with the equine misfortunes he'd witnessed in his time. 'I heard your lot thundering about last night,' he said. 'Hopefully the mare hasn't made it worse.'

As Jade wondered how to reply to this pessimism, Becca's mum returned with the box of food, Michaela and David.

'Michaela, honey!' Mr Parry said, leaving the breakfast table to hug the coach. 'I always look forward to this time of year. How long have you been coming here now?'

'I think this is the fifth year,' Michaela said, giving Mr Parry a peck on the cheek. 'How are you, Harry? You don't look any older than when I first brought a Flaxton team to stay.'

'Harry Parry?' David whispered to Jade; they were in the kitchen where they'd been put on toast and baked-beans duty. 'Really? What a name!'

Jade had to stop herself from snorting with laughter.

'What's funny?' Kristen said, having been sent to the kitchen to make hot drinks for everyone. She too started giggling when they told her.

'Is this hysteria due to lack of sleep or pre-competition nerves?' Michaela asked the giggling kitchen. 'Let's say both and hope that Mr Parry excuses you for rudely forgetting to ask whether he'd like another coffee or some toast. Would you, Harry?'

'I am a bit of a hobbit in the weekend,' he said, 'partial to a second breakfast. But I don't want to hold the young equestrians up.'

'The young equestrians,' Michaela said, 'would be more than happy to make you breakfast; it's the least they can do when you've been so kind as to billet them. And they're actually fairly organized. David, here — girls, I don't know if you've thanked him yet — has already caught the horses and given them each a little breakfast.'

Before tucking into their own breakfasts, the girls thanked David enthusiastically. Jade, who was always worrying about running late, calmed down a bit, and concentrated instead on not spilling baked beans down her front. She was in an old sweatshirt and track pants — every rider's pristine gear was hanging ready in the truck — so it didn't really matter, but being clumsy so early in the day seemed like a bad omen.

The hour after breakfast felt like five minutes; there was so much to do and remember. Becca's mum cleared away the breakfast dishes while the riders began grooming their already excited animals. David and Kristen were in good spirits, whistling 'Bohemian Rhapsody' together as they began plaiting.

'Can you stop that?' Amanda said. 'You're upsetting Blue.'

'That's funny, I'm sure the whistling's calming Johnny down,' Kristen said.

'Would you prefer it if we sang?' David asked Amanda, before launching into 'Galileo, Galileo!' Kristen joined in, and Jade was tempted to as well, amused by Amanda's bright-red face, but Michaela told them to stop.

'Cut out that racket for a minute, would you?' She and Mr Parry were scrutinizing Medusa's gait as Corina trotted her out.

'Bit stiff, do you think?' Michaela asked Mr Parry. Her arms were crossed and lips pursed.

'You're imagining things,' he said after a while. 'If you hadn't told me it was the off-hind, I'd never have known.'

'Honestly?' Corina said, relieved. 'I can ride her, then?'

'Up to your coach,' he said, patting Michaela's shoulder. 'But, as far as I can see, it's just a scratch. She'll be jumping as happy as ever in a few hours, I'd say.'

Michaela let out a long sigh. 'OK, then. But, if she's favouring that fetlock after her first round, she's out. I'd hate to ruin the team, but I'd hate even more to ruin your mare, Corina.'

On the dot of seven-thirty the three ponies and three horses were looking immaculate. As Jade velcroed the last travel boot onto Dorian's spotless off-hind leg, getting hoof oil on her nervous hands in the process while dodging the pony's cantankerous tail-swishes, she heard a commotion at Becca's truck. Medusa, remembering yesterday's trauma, was refusing to load.

'Let's not dither,' Michaela said decisively, after two attempts to chase the mare up the ramp. 'Amanda, load Blue instead. Hopefully our truck won't have such negative associations.'

'If she boots Dorian or Johnny, there will be hell to

pay,' Kristen said to Jade, unfortunately in Corina's earshot.

'I'm sorry she's such a witch!' Corina said, upset. 'But there's nothing I can do about it. She's a sweet jumper and fine with people — she's just stink at making friends.'

Seeing Corina's embarrassment, Kristen and Jade felt bad.

'She might be fine with our two,' Kristen said quickly. 'Try not to worry about it. I'm sorry I made a fuss.'

By some miracle, Kristen was right. Whether it was the smell of the Lewises' better-quality hay, or the example of blasé Dorian, who, already loaded on the truck, was resting a hind hoof and munching on the lucerne, or the fact that she was now the only horse left standing in the driveway, Medusa pulled herself together at last and trotted up the ramp.

'You'd better get a clear round, you dog!' Michaela shouted to the horse as she put the ramp up. Jade could tell Michaela was joking, but poor Corina's face had turned greenish-grey. She climbed into the cab of the truck, then twisted around to look through the back window, keeping an eye on the horses.

As the trucks departed in convoy, Mr Parry's yearlings in the paddock next to the driveway cantered after them along the fence line, graunching to an untidy halt when they reached the roadside.

The team hadn't driven far before they joined a procession of floats and trucks. 'Everyone seems to be going to the Champs,' Jade said nervously.

'You just wait until we get there,' Michaela said, grinning. 'It'll make the Flaxton Show look like a tiny gymkhana.'

Twenty minutes later, when they were unloading the horses, Jade saw what Michaela had meant. She felt suddenly small and shabby. At least Dorian looked at home here, Jade thought, with a pang of guilt for betraying Pip.

Instead of gazing around at the ponies, parents, riders and many shiny vehicles — let alone the terrifyingly professional-looking courses in the distance across the paddock — Jade set to work on Dorian, constantly watching out for her irritable teeth and hooves. Jade was glad of the cosy, familiar zone between Becca's truck and the Lewises'. Parked just far enough apart so that the tied-up horses weren't in kicking distance of each other, the trucks formed a little house. Becca's mum had even set up a picnic table in her truck — after the horses' droppings had been removed, of course.

Becca was fixing one of Dusty's plaits that had come unrolled during the journey. Satisfied with Dorian's gleaming silver coat and sufficiently tidy plaits, Jade gave the pony a quick kiss on the eyebrow before joining her friend.

'Dusty looks stunning,' Jade said, patting his shiny dun neck. 'Do you reckon we should go and walk the course soon?'

Becca grimaced. 'I guess so.'

'Why the long face?' Michaela said, coming over to them with a body brush in one hand and a stencil cut out with diamond shapes in the other. 'No, I'm not talking to you, Dusty!' Michaela grinned at her own terrible joke.

'Nervous,' Becca said, grimacing.

'Why?' Michaela asked, deftly holding the stencil against Dusty's rump and brushing over it sideways.

'Because it's such a big competition, and I don't want to let the team down,' Becca said.

'You've earned your place in the team, Becca; I wouldn't have chosen you if I didn't think you and Dusty could manage. There, isn't that smart?' Michaela had taken away the stencil, leaving a perfect diamond pattern on the pony's rump.

'You're living up to your name, old chap,' Michaela added as she stencilled his other hindquarter and was met with a small cloud of white dust.

Becca blushed. 'Sorry! I thought I'd shampooed that out the day before yesterday, and he's been wearing his cover since then.'

'Don't worry,' Michaela laughed. 'Rumps are hard to get completely clean; I've seen far worse. Right, I think the junior team's mounts are looking splendid now, but the riders are very scruffy.'

Jade and Becca looked at each other. They were both in old track pants and sweatshirts. Jade's pants were stained with hoof oil and her sleeve had a green smear where Dorian had dribbled chewed chaff this morning. That seemed like a week ago now.

The girls got changed in Becca's truck. As Jade

was pulling on her new boots — a 'congratulations' present from her dad for getting selected for the team — Amanda, Kristen and Corina joined them.

'White jodhpurs make me look so fat,' Amanda complained, craning around, trying to stare at herself.

Kristen, who was tying a half-Windsor knot in her navy-blue tie, rolled her eyes but didn't say anything.

'My feet *feel* so fat in my boots,' Becca said, mimicking Amanda's voice and making Corina laugh.

'It's true, though,' Becca said. 'The boots feel way smaller than when I last wore them.'

'What's wrong?' Becca's mum asked, tidying away the grooming tools.

My boots are too small,' Becca said, in a voice that made her mother sigh deeply.

'I am certain I asked you after the Elsemere Sports Day whether you needed new ones. Remember, you said they were too tight then?'

Becca grumpily agreed.

'Well, there's nothing we can do about them now. You're just going to have to grit your teeth and bear it.'

Hobbling down to the course, Becca seemed too preoccupied with her feet to admire the beautifully painted jumps. Instead she was peering at the line of stalls selling saddlery, hard feed and back protectors. None of them sold boots.

'Look,' Jade said, pointing at a pony standing on a low metal platform. 'I think that's a big set of scales, for weighing horses.' She hoped this novelty would distract Becca.

'You can weigh the ponies as much as you like *after* you've each had a clear round,' Michaela said sternly. 'Focus on the course for now. You know the deal here? There won't be a jump-off, so the idea is not only to go clear, but to floor the accelerator, too.'

They studied the plan of the course, which was tacked to the judges' truck. 'It's long,' Becca commented. 'Twelve jumps, including a triple!'

'And twisty,' Jade added. 'That turn from four onto five is nasty.'

Michaela swept their concerns away with a contemptuous wave of her hand. 'Nothing you can't manage; this is exactly what we've been practising for over the last six weeks. I don't want to hear any more snivelling. You're great little riders, with clever ponies, so positive thoughts from here on in.'

Becca had to stifle a yelp of horror at the first fence, a beautiful 85-centimetre oxer, quite wide and painted black and white. The panel at the front was decorated with musical notes and there was a pot of *Buxus* beside each of the jump stands.

'It's like something from the Horse of the Year Show,' Jade said, trying to sound impressed rather than nervous. 'Look at the plants!'

'The pot plants are great,' Michaela said. 'They act as wings, directing the horse to the centre of the jump. A very inviting first fence, if you ask me.'

Becca gulped silently as they walked around the rest of the course, following the line that they would aim to ride and measuring the strides with their own paces. Each jump seemed more elaborate than the last, with the final triple having a buzzy-bee theme. Jump C in the triple, a 90-centimetre upright, actually had a large wooden model of a buzzy bee as its filler. Jade and Becca gasped in unison.

'It's horrible!' Becca said.

'Shh, you'll offend the course designer,' Michaela scolded.

'But it's so off-putting,' Becca argued.

'Not if you think about it in the context of the whole course,' Michaela reasoned. 'Look, it's the last in a triple, so, if you get the stride right at jump A, the rest should be a piece of cake. Dusty will be in the swing of things, hopefully, and will barely even notice the decoration, unless, of course, you get all tense and distract him from his job.'

'Also,' Jade said, wanting to calm Becca, too, 'it's facing the practice arena, so we'll be jumping towards other horses. If you like, I could stand right there with Dorian.'

'No! You'll put me off,' Becca said.

'Jade has a point, though, doesn't she?' Michaela said, patting Becca's tense shoulder. 'Relax, you'll be fine.'

Looking at her watch, Michaela told the girls it was time to get into the saddle and start warming up. She'd meet them at the junior practice arena in fifteen minutes, after walking the intermediate course with Amanda and Kristen.

Jade was getting a leg-up from David when Becca's mum yelled from the truck: 'Wait! Just a minute!' Jade and David looked at each other, baffled.

'Helmet off,' Becca's mum ordered. 'Your hair is all over the place, young lady.'

David made a sympathetic face at Jade as her hair was pulled tightly back into a bun, then covered with a brown hairnet, which was pinned securely into place.

'There, isn't that better?' Becca's mum said, watching Jade gingerly feeling the back of her head.

'I guess,' Jade agreed, secretly thinking how itchy it would be under her helmet.

'Doesn't it look better, David?' Becca's mum asked, wanting backup.

'Oh, yes!' he said in a silly voice. 'It's fabulous.'

'It's all right for you — you don't have to wear one,' Jade whispered to David as he legged her up.

When their appearance satisfied Becca's mum, Jade and Becca walked briskly to the junior practice area, where the jumps and the riders looked comfortingly small.

Trotting in a circle together now, they witnessed a nasty crash at the practice jump. A girl, who looked about ten, was clinging to her bay for dear life.

'Bring him around again, and smack him this time!' yelled a woman in sunglasses who was standing next to the jump.

The girl did as she was told, but to no avail. The sweaty gelding once again tried to duck out to the side. This time the woman in sunglasses was ready. She made a fist and punched the horse hard in the cheek.

'That'll teach you, ya clown!' she growled.

'Don't, Mum!' the girl cried. The child's hairnet had come loose and was hanging wispily behind her ear.

'Poor thing,' Jade said.

'The girl or the pony?' Becca asked.

Keeping away from the jump until the problem pony had gone, Jade and Becca trotted and cantered on either rein. Dorian was slightly hotter than usual, spooking at a gust of wind. Dusty, however, seemed uncharacteristically calm. The crowds of ponies and promise of showjumping suited him.

'They're looking lovely,' Michaela called, walking across to meet her youngest charges. 'There's time for a couple of practice jumps, Jade, then you're on!'

Jade shortened her reins and pushed her heels even further down. She was ready.

A Clean Break

Easy, girl,' Jade said, sliding her palm down Dorian's neck and shoulder as they waited for the steward to let them into the ring. Perfect pony or not, Dorian was unfamiliar; Jade tried not to think about Pip at home in Mr White's yard. If only she were riding Pip now, instead of Kristen's carefully schooled showjumping machine on which, if Jade were honest, she was more of a passenger than a pilot.

'Number 18: Jade Lennox on Dorian, riding for Flaxton District Pony Clubs,' said a woman over the loudspeaker, with a voice like the Briscoe's lady.

'Good luck, dear,' the steward said, letting Jade into the ring after a stocky appaloosa, who'd been unlucky in knocking a rail off the precarious triple bar, jogged out. His rider was grinning and patting him vigorously nonetheless.

Jade had barely gathered up the reins before Dorian was cantering eagerly past the truck. For a sickening moment, Jade thought she'd forgotten to check her girth. Was the saddle slipping? No; David had taken it up another two notches after giving her a leg-up. Her gear was fine; she just had to concentrate now.

They were coming around to the flags, a little too fast for Jade's liking, but she trusted Dorian. The ears in front of her, smaller and pointier than Pip's, were pricked and alert. The stride, drumming evenly at the ground beneath them, was shorter than Pip's, but full of impulsion. They met the musical-notes oxer bang on the mark.

Leaning forward, with a handful of plait in her right hand and her whip in the left, Jade looked for the next jump in mid-air. Dorian recognized the subtle turn of her rider's body and was on the right leg and beginning to bend as soon as she'd landed. *Where's the next one?* the pony asked, with one ear back, listening to Jade's hands and legs. *The rainbow triple bar*, Jade replied, sitting back deep in the saddle for three strides, aiming her experienced steed for the indigo stripe right in the middle of the poles.

Jade grimaced as Dorian took off too far out for her liking. Leaning right forward, giving the pony plenty of rein, she hoped that Dorian's back hooves wouldn't take the top rail with them. However, accustomed to jumps 30 centimetres higher than these, Dorian knew what she was doing and landed cleanly.

'Clever, girl!' Jade breathed, giving Dorian's neck a brisk pat as they charged across the ring towards the pale pink upright. *Too fast*, Jade thought, sitting up and using the muscles in her back and shoulders to collect the excited pony. *One, two, three*, Jade silently counted the strides to a perfect takeoff.

'Just the triple now,' Jade whispered, steering the show-jumper very tightly around the last corner but straightening up in time to meet the last three jumps squarely. As Michaela had predicted, the pony was too focused on the gymnastic effort of the course to even notice the giant buzzy-bee filler in jump C.

Skidding slightly as they raced through the finish

flags, Jade pounded Dorian's neck with pats. 'Good girl! Very good girl!'

It was a clear round; a fast, clear round.

Jade was elated and tired as she brought Dorian back to a walk. At the ringside, Becca was grinning widely and gave the thumbs-up when she caught Jade's eye. Becca's mum, Michaela and Kristen were waiting, too. Theirs were the only smiling faces nearby; everyone else seemed, to Jade, nervous or resentful.

'Good round,' the next rider said, before cattily adding, 'by the pony, I mean. Anyone could go clear on Dorian.' His eyes were pale blue, his face very pink and clean, his expression unpleasant. Jade didn't know what to say, which didn't matter because the boy had already spurred his own pony on in a flashy way. The dish-nosed Arab kicked up a clod of dirt as they cantered past the truck.

'Do you know who that was?' Jade asked Kristen, who had ridden over on a fidgety Johnny to congratulate her pony and team-mate.

'Yannick Van de Meer, from Gorsewood Pony Club. He's super competitive,' Kristen said.

Jade told her Yannick's remark, making Kristen laugh. 'What a dork! He's just worried you'll beat him. And I reckon you will. Man, Dozz loved that, Jade! Thanks for giving her such a good ride,' said Kristen.

'She was so good,' Jade replied, dry-mouthed. 'It was a really fun round. Thank you so much for letting me borrow her. And Yannick's right: it was mostly her.'

'No,' said Michaela, who'd overheard their conversation, 'he's not right. Dorian's a very tidy show-jumper, but she's not a push-button pony. I'd bet that he couldn't have gone as fast *and clear* as you did. Look at those heavy hands,' Michaela said, gesturing at Yannick as he pulled his pony around to the triple bar. 'Is he really wearing pale blue string gloves?'

Kristen burst out laughing. 'They match his tie and saddle blanket.'

A tall blonde woman turned round and glared at Michaela. 'I would've thought you'd be more professional,' she said slowly.

Michaela looked chastened. 'Frieda, I'm sorry; I didn't see you there.'

Frieda Van de Meer breathed in through her nose,

put on her sunglasses and turned back to watch her son.

'Right, I think it'd be a good time to get you ready for your round,' Michaela said quickly to Kristen. 'Jade, you can take Dorian back to the truck — both of you deserve a break and a bite to eat.'

'I thought I might stay and watch Becca,' Jade said. 'She's only three riders away; aren't you, Bec?'

Becca nodded sadly.

'Don't pull that face!' Jade said, laughing. 'You'll be fine.'

'I know we should be fine,' Becca said, 'But my feet really hurt; whenever I put my heels down, it's agony. I can't concentrate on riding.'

Becca's mum rolled her eyes and sighed. 'We've been through this — you're going to have to just deal with it for now, unless we cut the toes out right here. I'll try and find a shop after your round and buy a larger pair for this afternoon. It's the best I can do, Becca.'

'You could borrow my boots,' Jade suggested. 'My feet are a bit bigger than yours.'

'There! Problem solved,' Michaela said. 'Good

luck, Becca. We're off now. I'll see you at the truck afterwards.'

'Good luck to you too,' Becca said to Kristen. 'Not that you'll need it.'

'Oh, you'd better believe I'll need it on Johnny,' Kristen said. 'He's green as grass.'

'C'mon, daughter — you're catching Becca's pessimism,' Michaela said. 'See you littlies later.'

Becca, who was already off Dusty's back and trying on Jade's lovely new boots, grinned. She and Jade were used to Michaela's teasing now.

'They fit, Mum! They're perfect!' Becca said, delightedly walking back and forth as far as Dusty's reins would let her.

'Thank you very much, Jade. You've saved the day. Make sure you watch your feet around all these ponies with studs in their shoes,' Becca's mum warned, taking her nervous daughter for one last practice jump.

Jade decided to stay and watch the competition. Standing in her sweaty white socks, next to Dorian, who was now placidly resting a hind hoof and flicking her tail at flies, Jade felt that wonderful sense of relief and fatigue. She'd done well, and there was plenty of time until the next round. She could relax.

'And you can relax too, lovely girl,' Jade said to Dorian, allowing the pony to rub her head on Jade's shoulder, leaving a scattering of white hairs. Jade ran her stirrups up, loosened Dorian's girth, then watched the debacle of the next round. The girl whom Jade had seen crying at the practice jump and her mother who'd punched the poor bay in the face were tussling with the scared pony at the arena gate. 'Give him a proper smack, not a wussy tap on the neck. Belt him behind the bloody girth, girl!' the mother bellowed.

Jade could see the girl's eyes welling up again. Which team were they from? Jade wondered, examining the sky-blue jersey, saddle blanket and helmet cover. They were wearing the same colours as Yannick. Surely the Gorsewood team, which Michaela had warned would be very competitive, wouldn't treat a pony, and indeed a rider, like that?

'Poor girl,' Jade whispered into Dorian's mane, watching her short, weak legs flapping ineffectually at the pony's sides. 'Poor pony too; he's terrified.'

The bay had the same dished face as Yannick's

chestnut, Speculaas, but its body was less refined. It looked more like a little station-bred horse than a pony, Jade thought; but, more to the point, it looked frantic. His nostrils were flared, eyes wild and ears pinned back. Both pony and rider were terrified and angry — perhaps not at each other so much as the situation. Both seemed confused about what was required of them.

'Hit him! For crying out loud!' the mother yelled again, watching her daughter's pony start to spin back around towards the gate. Doing as she was told, the girl gave her pony a mighty thwack on his stomach with her whip. The judge, sitting in the truck, shook his head and put the bell back down, giving the pair another minute to collect themselves.

'It won't work!' the girl squealed, as the pony shot forward then graunched to a halt again, seeing the mother filling the arena gateway, fists clenched. With the curb chain tight behind his chin, the whip flailing around his head now, and the girl on his back thumping up and down, the bay rose on his hind legs — there was nowhere else for him to go. With the reins clumped along with his mane so tightly in her sore hands, the rider, screaming, pulled her rearing pony up higher. 'Mum!' the girl howled. 'He's going backwards!'

'Lean forward! Drop the reins!' another mother was shouting now, seeing the catastrophe before it happened. But the terrified child wouldn't let go. Jade thought of the description of the rearing horse in *Oliver Twist* — but this was much worse, not remotely funny. Not wanting to watch but unable to look away, Jade saw the bay pony's hind legs slip out from under him as he fell backwards. The girl, who'd lost both stirrups now, with impressive presence of mind — or at least instinct — finally let go of the mane and reins, allowing her to fall to the side instead of getting pinned under the weight of her pony. There was still a sickening moment when both the girl and the pony seemed to be trying to get to their feet at once, the pony's hooves dangerously close to the girl's slight body.

'I'm gonna take him home and shoot him!' the mother bellowed, running to her daughter's side and ignoring the pony, who, stirrups swinging at his side and reins trailing, was bolting from the arena.

'Here, boy!' Jade called without thinking, holding the barely interested Dorian with her right hand and reaching for the bay's reins with her left. The pony came to her with surprising obedience. As Jade got a good handful of his reins, she saw the manic pony barrel into poor Dorian's side and felt his freshly shod hoof crush through her thin sock.

Jade heard her own scream but didn't recognize her voice. She was too distracted by that sick ache behind her eyes which came with intense pain. She'd felt this before when she'd fallen off Pip, but not to the same extent. Hopping on one foot, holding both Dorian's and the manic pony's reins, Jade began to feel faint. She thought she'd have to sit down quite soon. *At least he's settled now*, she thought, watching the bay nuzzling at Dorian, who seemed to get on with all ponies. *They won't trample me if I sit down*, Jade thought, falling backwards and blacking out.

'Jade! What happened to you, sweet? Jade?' Becca's mum was hovering over her, pulling her up and stroking her back. 'Sweetheart, I told you to watch your feet!'

'That pony was running away. Where's it gone?'

'The owner took it away; the girl was upset after her fall and the mother was set on beating the pony to a pulp by the sounds of it. Oh, good — you'll be OK now, love,' Becca's mum said, seeing the St John's ambulance pull up slowly, and the crowd of ponies and riders part.

'Yep, you've definitely broken it,' the paramedic said cheerfully, holding the rapidly swelling foot in its stained sock. 'Let's get you to A&E and put a cast on it.'

Jade, still feeling faint, was lifted into the back of the ambulance.

'What about Dorian?' Jade asked, seeing that Becca's mum was coming with her.

'Corina's taken her back to the truck. She'll be fine.'

'What about Becca?'

'Becca's just finished her round — she went clear too!'

'Good,' Jade said, closing her eyes. 'Thanks for coming with me.'

Becca's mum, who was still rubbing Jade's back, trying to distract her from the pain, smiled wearily.

At the hospital, Jade didn't have to wait long before the paramedic and Becca's mum helped her onto a bed behind a curtain, where a doctor was ready to X-ray her foot.

'Horses,' he said sternly, shaking his head as he gently snipped off her sock and cut a split in her good jodhpurs. 'Dangerous creatures. You show-jumpers are going to keep me very busy today; I can feel it.'

Jade mumbled an apology and closed her eyes. The paramedic had given her something for the pain, which was successfully numbing everything below her left ankle. The pain all seemed to be in her head now, muzzy and constant, like car sickness.

She opened her eyes again and saw the doctor disinfecting the skin the hoof had broken, in preparation for the cast. Where was Becca's mum?

'I'm right here, Jade.'

Jade didn't even realize she'd called. 'Oh, OK.'

'I've just called your dad, and Michaela. Your dad's

driving up right now, he says. Though I told him you'd survive.'

'Driving?' Jade's dad had ridden a bicycle ever since the accident. Maybe Granddad would drive him, but that would leave the garage unattended. Granddad prided himself on opening on Sundays. Jade felt like a nuisance. Why had she grabbed that pony's reins?

'Yep; he said he'd leave right away. I told him to wait until tomorrow — it'll be midnight by the time he gets here — but he insisted. I suppose I'd be the same if it were Becca or Matthew.'

Jade could feel the cold, wet plaster wrapping around her foot now. She didn't want to look, though; last time she'd peeked down, it had looked more like an eggplant than a foot. But she'd be alright now. She was being looked after.

'I won't get a boot on over the cast,' Jade said sadly, making Becca's mum laugh. 'Is Michaela very angry?'

'Disappointed, but not at you, sweet. She knows it was just bad luck.'

'I've ruined the team. It's like we were cursed; first Pip going lame, now me.'

'You've had really shocking luck, I know. But it's not the end of the world. The Jigsaw event is out of the question, but if the others do well we're still in with a chance.'

Jade looked grim. If she'd just gone back to the truck with Dorian, or stayed on Dorian's back when her boots were off, none of this would've happened.

'Oh, and Michaela had some news that should cheer you up,' Becca's mum said, seeing Jade's serious face. 'You and Dorian won the first event; Yannick was a close second, and Becca was third. Good result, eh?'

The plaster was dry now, and Jade was handed a pair of crutches.

'You look like a sensible girl,' the doctor said, peering over the top of his glasses. 'I don't have to remind you to keep off your pony's back for the next six weeks, do I?'

'That won't be a problem,' Jade said glumly. 'My pony's lame anyway, and I'll have to give back the one I've been borrowing.'

'Jolly good,' the doctor said, with no apparent empathy for Pip. 'Where did you say you were from again?'

'Flaxton.'

'I think there's an A&E there?'

'Yeah, I got my wrist fixed there last year.'

'Of course you did,' the doctor said. 'Riders are always in the wars. Well, they can take your cast off after four weeks. Would you like to keep the X-ray?'

Jade looked at the white branches of bone stretching down to her toes. The branch leading to her big toe had splintered in the middle, and the bone had a tiny gap, like a strand of hair.

'Yes, please!' She could pin it on her wall next to Pip's X-ray.

'Right, who's my next equestrian casualty?' the doctor called callously. Jade thought he was joking, but then saw another girl about her age stagger in wearing grass-stained jodhpurs and cradling her arm.

It was a long hobble on the crutches out to the taxi Becca's mum had ordered.

'Are you sure you don't want to go back to Mr Parry's and have a proper sleep?' she asked, in a motherly tone that Jade enjoyed.

'No, I want to be with the others,' Jade said. 'I can rest in the back of your truck if I need to.'

'Fair enough,' Becca's mum agreed. 'But careful around the horses, and gumboot on at all times. If your other foot goes, you'll need a wheelchair rather than just crutches!'

Taniwha

The little cripple's back!' David said, as the taxi drove away slowly, so as not to scare the horses.

'David, don't use that word,' Becca's mum scolded.

'Sorry,' he said unconvincingly. 'You OK, Jade?'

'Yep, not too bad,' she said, realizing the sock on her good foot was slipping down around her heel.

The rest of the team was sitting on the ramps of each truck, eating steak sandwiches and chips from the hot-food caravan, and fruit from the chilly bin Becca's mum had thoughtfully packed. The horses and ponies were untacked and permitted to nibble on the hay-nets for ten minutes, as there was still an hour until the next event.

'Are you hungry, Jade? Shall I pop down and get you a steak sammie?' Michaela asked.

'Maybe a punnet of chips?' Jade asked. Her stomach was churning, and she couldn't tell if it was from hunger or pain.

'Right you are. Get yourself comfortable and I'll be back soon.'

Sitting in the sun on the ramp, with her crutches by her side, Becca and Kristen brought Jade up to date on the current scores.

'So, you won obviously, which is fantastic,' Kristen said, ducking into the cab of the truck and grabbing the pile of sashes that had been hung over the rear-view mirror. 'Here, Jade, this one's yours.' Kristen passed her a lavish, wide red ribbon. 'And this one's Becca's,' Kristen went on, untangling a yellow sash from the bundle. 'She was only a second behind Yannick, which is amazing.'

'And Kristen got fourth with Johnny,' Becca said, pointing at the green sash.

'I got second,' Amanda cut in, with little modesty. Her own blue ribbon was rolled up neatly and sitting in her helmet.

'David's our hero, though,' Corina continued, before anyone could give Amanda a withering look. 'He won the senior event.'

'How did you do?' Jade asked Corina.

'Not so flash — we got sixth.'

'Any placing is a great achievement here,' Becca's mum said. 'Was Medusa's fetlock alright?'

'I'm convinced she's a bit stiff and out of sorts, but Michaela swears that Mr Parry would have noticed if she was actually lame,' Corina said.

'Anyway, the main thing is that we're currently coming second to Gorsewood,' Kristen said, with a big mouthful of apple. 'We're in with a chance!'

'Even without me?' Jade said, then blushed, realizing how vain that sounded.

'It *is* looking good, despite the scratching of Jade Lennox,' David said. 'The pony that stomped on your foot belongs to Gorsewood. They're unlikely to get placed in anything, so we're pretty much equal with our rivals.'

Jade nodded, trying to take this in, but mainly just feeling the heavy, pulsing weight of her cast.

'Why is that girl in the Gorsewood team? I thought

they were a good pony club,' Amanda said.

Michaela, who'd just handed Jade a punnet of chips and patted her on the shoulder as if she were a co-operative pony, answered Amanda's question. 'I just bumped into Frieda at the food caravan and we talked about just that. It seems that their gun junior had to pull out — dislocated her shoulder last week — and Loretta Sand was their only other option,' she said in a stage whisper, worried that a Gorsewood team member would ride past and hear her gossiping.

'Loretta had a push-button first pony, apparently,' Michaela continued, 'but her mum has just bought her this five-year-old and they can't do a thing with him. Frieda is livid.'

'If I were Frieda I'd have strongly suggested that Mrs Sand stay at home,' Becca's mum said.

'The Sands are quite good for sponsorship — without them Gorsewood pony club wouldn't have a brand-new set of jump stands. Frieda's trying to educate Mrs Sand, so far without success.'

'Poor Loretta,' Becca sighed.

'And that poor pony,' Jade added.

'The brute that crushed your foot?' Kristen asked. 'Man, you're forgiving, Jade.'

Ignoring Becca's mum's suggestion to have a lie down in the truck bunk, Jade insisted on watching Becca's round in the next event.

'Well, I'm bringing you a deck chair,' Becca's mum said. 'And once we're at the ring, you're to sit down and *rest*.'

'I could sit on Dorian; she'd probably like to watch, too.'

Becca's mum stared at Jade. 'Did you not listen to that doctor? No riding for six weeks!'

'I was joking,' Jade said quickly, although, having suggested the ride, she now wanted it. Poor Dorian, left alone at the trucks, all finished for the day. Kristen had kindly sluiced her down, unplaited her mane, put a travel sheet on and given her a feed. Perhaps Jade was imagining things, but to her Dorian seemed slightly hurt. She was always the one competing, never the one left behind. And now, here she was, all finished for the day and looking like her mane had been permed, while the other horses were still spotless and ready to perform.

Michaela and Becca had gone ahead to have another warm-up at the practice jump, while Becca's mum and Jade followed at a snail's pace due to Jade's inexperience with the crutches.

Reluctant to rush Jade, but also not wanting to miss her daughter's round, Becca's mum was visibly relieved when a man on a quad bike pulled up and offered some assistance.

'You're not one of these hoons that'll roll us over, are you?' Becca's mum asked, laughing. The driver wouldn't have been a day under fifty and drove extremely cautiously.

'No, that'd be my son that you're describing,' the man replied. 'I like a more leisurely pace.'

Jade was grateful for this; even driving slowly over the undulating paddock sent hot pulses of pain through her foot. It was lovely to finally sit still in a deck chair next to Becca's mum, with a perfect view of the course. Without the disappointment of not being able to compete, Jade's afternoon would've been almost perfect. The day was clear and still, but not baking hot or glaringly bright — perfect conditions for showjumping.

From her ringside seat, Jade could see that the course had been rearranged. Becca would be nervously complaining, and Michaela would be repeating the same calming words. *You've done this before; you can do it again. Dusty is more than capable. None of the jumps is any higher than those we've practised over. You are a good rider. Take it easy; slow and clear for now.* Yes, there would be a jump-off, which Dorian would almost certainly have got into. Jade tried to stop feeling regretful.

'Oh no, they're not trying again, are they?' Becca's mum suddenly whispered to Jade. 'Look who the first competitor is.'

'Poor Loretta,' Jade sighed.

'I hope everyone near the gate has their shoes on,' Becca's mum said. 'That pony's a liability.'

'He's got a jump on him though. Look!' Jade pointed.

For some reason, Loretta's difficult pony had now made up his mind to co-operate. Clearly, though, this decision had nothing to do with Loretta's riding: as the bay cleared the first oxer, tucking his knees up neatly, Loretta's own legs slid so far back that she was almost kneeling in the saddle. On landing, she lost a stirrup, but managed with a sudden jerk on the rein to steer her pony round to the next jump, a purple upright.

'Sit back; heels down; slow down!' Becca's mum was hissing inadvertently. Yet even if Loretta had heard, she didn't seem capable of performing any of these actions. The only reason she was staying in the saddle was the large handful of unrolled plaits to which she was clinging.

Free to charge flat-out at the purple jump — or baulk, or run out — the nervy bay pony made an uncharacteristically good decision. Two strides out, he slowed his pace and, without any contribution from his rider, took off perfectly.

'You're right: that pony's got some talent,' Becca's mum agreed. 'But little Loretta is really struggling.'

Having managed valiantly to clear the second jump with only one stirrup, Loretta lost her other stirrup on the corner to the third jump. Bouncing in the saddle and clinging to her pony's black mane, the child, seeing the imposing buzzy-bee triple fast approaching, did what one should never do on horseback, however scared: she screamed. At that moment, the bay went from nervous excitement to panic. Too late to pull out from the triple, he graunched to a halt. Loretta cleared the toppling poles without her pony, landing remarkably well on the far side.

'She's had some practice at that, poor thing,' Becca's mum said. 'And now that manic creature's off again.'

Jade watched him bolt past on the other side of the arena rope, but this time, instead of reaching for his rein, she pulled her broken foot well back under the deck chair.

'He's going to get tangled up in the rope; he'll burn his legs and frighten all the other ponies,' Becca's mum worried, reminding Jade where Becca's nerves came from.

'I think he's gonna jump it,' Jade said quietly. A few seconds later, the bay bounded over the rope as if it weren't there.

'Stop that pony!' Mrs Sand bellowed, chasing the bay with an unexpected turn of speed.

As he'd done the first time, the bay stopped of his

own accord when he joined a group of ponies, whose riders' feet were safely in their stirrups.

'Thanks, girls,' Jade heard Mrs Sand say before she yanked at the bay's reins. 'What was that for, you silly dog?' she shouted at the pony. 'You like terrorizing my daughter, do you?' As if waiting for the pony to reply, she jerked the bay's reins again, before delivering a vicious kick to his belly. The pony shuddered and snorted.

'Mum! Stop it!' Loretta sobbed, running over now, followed by the junior-ring steward. The steward spoke too quietly for Jade or Becca's mum to hear what she said, but they could guess from Mrs Sand's strident response.

'He could've killed my daughter, and you're complaining about a bit of discipline? Get your flipping priorities right! He deserves to be shot — I won't even be able to sell him on after this. My conscience wouldn't let me even *give* this beast to another child.'

'She's not really going to shoot him?' Jade asked Becca's mum.

'I hope not, Jade. But I do hope they get rid of him. Each day he gets beaten up by that woman, he'll become harder to salvage. It's such a shame. In fact, it makes me sick.'

It made Jade sick, too. Throughout Becca's excellent clear round, which even earned applause from Frieda Van de Meer, Jade could only think about the bay's neatly tucked-up knees, and the way he'd shuddered at Mrs Sand's kick.

'I think I'll have to go back to the truck and lie down for a bit; I'm feeling quite sore,' Jade said to Becca's mum, Michaela and Becca as they all walked to the intermediate ring to watch Amanda's round.

'I knew you were looking pale!' Becca's mum said, triumphant. 'Do you want me to come with you?'

'Nah, I'll be fine thanks. Got used to the crutches now.'

'Good luck, you guys!' Jade called to Amanda and Kristen, who had just finished at the practice jump. Kristen saluted in reply.

Jade hadn't been lying when she said her foot was sore, but it wasn't so sore that she couldn't have a little look for the Sands' truck. It wasn't hard to find, as the only truck larger than it was the Van de Meers', and that was parked right next door.

Inside the shiny beige truck, which had *GOLDEN SANDS BAR & GRILL* painted on the side with a gaudy cartoon of a chicken wearing sunglasses and holding a cocktail, Jade could hear crying.

'Well, do you want to keep him?' Mrs Sand asked.

'No,' Jade thought she heard, between sobs.

'Do you even want to keep riding?'

'I dunno.'

'I know you love him as a pet, darling, but he could kill you. He's dangerous. I'm not keeping him if we're always going to be afraid of him — and, really, I've run out of ideas. He's useless.'

'He was good for Tina,' Loretta said, having blown her nose and pulled herself together a bit.

'Tina's practically a criminal, selling him to us. Yes, he went fine for her, but no one else has managed to do anything with him. That girl was just tough as nails — no wonder she's riding track work now. Anyway, I'm not going to be responsible if he puts his next rider in a wheelchair. It'd just be safer to have him put down.'

'No!' Loretta wailed again. 'Could we just give him to someone and tell them everything. Maybe he needs to be broken in again?'

'Who is going to bother with him after this sorry performance today?' Mrs Sand asked, exasperated.

Jade, who'd been eavesdropping without any subtlety outside the truck, couldn't help piping up: 'Um, hello?'

'Who's there?' Mrs Sand asked sharply, striding down the truck's ramp. 'Oh no, it's that poor little girl Taniwha injured this morning. See, Loretta? He's already put someone in hospital today. See?'

Loretta looked like she was going be sick. She stood behind her mother, saying nothing.

'I'm so sorry about your foot,' Mrs Sand said. 'Is there anything we can do? Compensation?'

'Um, no. It's fine,' Jade said, unsure of where to start. 'It's just — well, I heard you talking about the pony just now, as I was walking past,' Jade added hurriedly, not wanting to admit to eavesdropping, 'and I'd like to take him, if you really want to get rid of him. I'd buy him.'

Mrs Sand looked confused. 'Is this a joke? Are you making fun of Loretta?'

'No, of course not!' Jade said. 'I know he's a really difficult pony, but in that last round, when I saw him jumping, I thought he could make a great pony one day. I'd hate it if he got put down.'

'What makes you think you'd do better with Taniwha than Loretta?'

Jade looked worried, not wanting to offend the mother and daughter standing before her.

'I don't doubt your riding skills,' Mrs Sand went on, almost kindly. 'I'd just never forgive myself if I read in the paper that a half-Kaimanawa half-Arab 14.2-hand bay gelding had killed a girl out hunting. I just want to be reassured, that's all.'

'I'll be fine!' Jade blurted out, not at all sure of whether she would be. 'I have great riding instructors, and I'm quite experienced now.'

'With five-year-olds?'

'I'll have lots of support.'

'Well, if you can show me some of this support, I'll think about letting you have Taniwha. I like horses as much as the next person, so I'd rather see him go to a good home than get put down, but he's just completely beyond me — sometimes he even seems evil.'

He didn't look evil to Jade; tied up next to one of the other Gorsewood horses, he looked defeated. There was still a sweaty saddle mark on his back and he had no hay-net.

'My dad will be here tomorrow. If he agrees, will you let me take Taniwha? I'd pay!' Jade said decisively.

'OK, sure; I'll talk to your dad tomorrow. But no, there's absolutely no need to pay.'

'No need to pay for what?' Yannick Van de Meer asked, dismounting from a sweaty Speculaas. 'Hey, you're that girl who was riding Kristen's pony until Taniwha crippled you. Good job, eh?'

'Yannick!' Mrs Sand scolded.

'Jeez, I was joking,' Yannick said.

'She wants Taniwha,' Loretta said, in a small husky voice.

'Wow!' Yannick said, taking his pony's bridle off and slipping on a halter. 'Are you mad?'

'I like him,' Jade said.

'Go for it, then. At least you won't beat me when you're riding him, eh?' Yannick laughed. 'Hey, can you ask your team-mate on the dun pony if she'd like to do the Jigsaw with me tomorrow? It makes sense because you're obviously out, and everyone agrees Loretta's not riding any more — right, Loretta?' Loretta nodded feebly, making Jade feel sorry for her again. 'Mum even reckons our teams might be allowed to split the points if we win.' He grinned as he pulled off his sky-blue gloves.

Jade was taken aback. Yannick talked so fast, and it was often hard to tell if he was being serious or not. 'Um, I'll ask Becca about it.'

'Cool, thanks.'

By the time Jade had hobbled back to the trucks on her crutches, she was genuinely feeling like a lie down. Dorian, who'd been dozing in the late afternoon sun, looked up and snickered gently. Before hoisting herself onto the truck's bunk, Jade found a horse mint in her grooming kit and gave it to the patient pony.

It felt like she'd only closed her eyes for five minutes when Jade was woken by the return of her teammates. Reaching for her crutches, Jade sat up and eased herself slowly off the bunk. She could hear excited voices and the familiar creaking and rattling of untacking.

'Jade, I got second!' Becca called, beaming. Dusty, who was drinking noisily from his bucket, was all untacked except for the pretty blue sash still tied round his neck.

'Well done!' Jade said, trying not to sound envious. She couldn't help wondering where she and Dorian would've been placed.

'It was the best jump-off we've ever done — eh, Mum?'

'Yep, you rode beautifully, and Dusty went like the clappers,' Becca's mum said, beginning to unplait Dusty's mane.

'How are the others doing?' Jade asked.

'The senior ring is still going; David and Corina both got into the jump-off, which is fantastic,' Becca's mum said.

'And Kristen and Amanda are waiting to hear the results,' Becca said, taking off her helmet and carefully untangling her hairnet. 'Mum watched Amanda's jump-off and thought it was fast.'

'My word, that Blue can motor around a course!'

Becca's mum said. 'I'd be very surprised if anyone beat their time. Though that Van de Meer girl — Yannick's older sister — might have given them a run for their money.'

'Did Yannick win the junior event?' Jade asked Becca.

'Yeah, it was a close one again. And he's not actually that bad — he congratulated me this time.'

'Oh, that's right,' Jade said, remembering. 'He asked me to ask you if you'd like to do the Jigsaw with him tomorrow. Apparently his mum reckons our teams could split the points if you get placed.'

Becca's face lit up. 'Really? When did you see him?'

'Just as I was walking back to the truck.' Jade blushed faintly, not wanting to have to explain her rash decision just yet.

'What do you think, Mum?' Becca asked.

'Why not? It'd be a shame to miss the last event. Shall we go and see if Yannick's at his truck, plan for tomorrow?'

While Becca and her mum went to visit the Gorse-wood team, Jade was left to keep an eye on Dusty and Dorian. Running her fingers through Dusty's ridiculously curly mane, Jade worried: about her offer to take Taniwha, about poor Pip — whom she'd hardly thought about all day — and about her dad on the long drive from Flaxton. He hadn't driven since the accident. He shouldn't be driving right now.

'You look deep in thought,' Kristen said, sliding tiredly off Johnny's back.

Jade jumped. 'I was miles away. Hey, well done!' Johnny, Jade saw now, had a handsome yellow sash around his neck.

'Thanks,' Kristen said. 'I'm really happy with Mr Sparrow today; a woman even asked if he was for sale after our jump-off. But the real stars are Blue and Amanda.'

Amanda, to her credit, couldn't stop making a fuss of Blueberry Tart. 'It was mostly down to her — she's never been so good,' Amanda said, hugging her horse's neck.

Blue and Johnny had their noses deep in their feed buckets by the time David and Corina returned, exhausted and elated from their jump-off.

'We'll have to celebrate tonight!' said Michaela, who'd been watching the end of the senior event. 'Our team has some of the best young show-jumpers in New Zealand, I'm convinced. David, two wins today! I'd tell you to give yourself a pat on the back if I didn't hate that phrase. And Amanda, stunning riding this afternoon: thoughtful and brave.'

'How did you go?' Jade whispered to Corina, as Michaela continued raving. Corina didn't say anything, but pulled a crumpled green sash out of her jacket pocket.

'Fourth's really good!' Jade said, trying not to sound condescending. 'Any placing is good — that's what Becca's mum said.'

Corina shook her head, disappointed. 'It's just not been our day. Medusa's beaten David and Toby before — I know we can do better than this. It's just frustrating letting the team down; Gorsewood were second and third behind David in both events today.'

'If anyone's let the team down, it's me,' Jade said, waving her cast at Corina. 'At least you weren't silly enough to try and catch a bolting horse in your bare feet.'

Corina laughed. 'I suppose not.'

That evening, the hard-working horses were turned out in the paddock before nightfall, and the hungry riders were allowed to celebrate with a barbecued feast.

Sitting outside, her polar fleece zipped up to her chin and a paper plate piled with steak, salad, bread and a corn cob, Jade felt pleasantly sleepy. Her dad had phoned to let her know that he was staying the night in Turangi, so there was no need to worry about him driving in the dark. And he'd been able to reassure her that Pip's condition wasn't any worse, and perhaps was even a little better.

Jade's one nagging worry was Taniwha. As her team-mates relived the day, describing each of their rounds to an entranced Mr Parry, Jade couldn't bring herself to mention the offer she'd made Mrs Sand. That could wait until tomorrow.

Two Ponies

Wearing track pants rather than jodhpurs, as they were easier to pull on over her cast, Jade did her best to be helpful on Sunday morning. But on crutches she wasn't much use at catching the horses, or even at carrying everyone's belongings to the trucks. In the end, she was left with Mr Parry to do the breakfast dishes.

'I think I've done something silly,' she said quietly to Mr Parry, as he washed and she dried.

'What's that then?' he asked, strangely unsurprised that this mousy girl had finally spoken to him.

'I offered to buy the pony that broke my foot.'

'The one you lot were talking about last night?'

Mr Parry asked. 'The one that reared and took off?'

Jade nodded.

'Why?' Mr Parry asked.

'He's a good jumper, and I like the look of him,' Jade said unconvincingly. 'And I don't want him to get shot.'

'Do you still want him today?' Mr Parry asked.

'I think so.'

'Then if I were you, I'd tell Michaela about it. She's got a top eye for a horse and will give you some good advice.'

Jade nodded, relieved that the first adult she'd told about Taniwha hadn't shouted at her.

When the dishes were finished, Jade hopped outside and helped Becca roll up the last of Dusty's plaits, and then it was time to go. The Flaxton team said their goodbyes and thank yous to Mr Parry. Kristen presented him with a beautifully wrapped bottle of tawny port.

'Oh, this is the nice stuff,' Mr Parry chuckled. 'You lot spoil me.'

He stood, waving the bottle at the riders and calling, 'See you next year, I hope!' and 'Good luck!'

as the trucks rolled slowly down the driveway.

At the showgrounds, everyone seemed busy, especially Michaela, whom Jade was desperate to consult about Taniwha. What with finding Johnny's lost tendon boot and convincing Corina that Medusa's fetlock wasn't at all stiff or swollen, Michaela had no time for the girl in track pants, a T-shirt and one gumboot, who was trying to keep her crutches out of the way.

'Michaela,' Jade called shyly, when the coach seemed to be between tasks.

'What is it, Jade? Becca and I were just about to find Yannick and walk the course. You should come, too.'

'Too late,' Jade whispered. From where she was standing on the ramp, she had a good view of the approaching Gorsewood team members. Yannick on Speculaas, flanked by Frieda, Mrs Sand and Loretta on foot. 'The Van de Meers are coming,' Jade said in a small voice.

'Good,' Michaela said. 'I wonder if Frieda's charmed the judges into letting us split points.'

Frieda had not managed to charm the judges. 'It's outrageous,' she said in a slow, deep voice. 'On the scoreboard we are clearly the winning teams already — you are slightly ahead, actually. The other teams are only competing for third. Outrageous,' she said again, savouring the word.

'Can't say I'm surprised,' Michaela said. 'It was hard enough persuading them to let Jade ride Dorian. Look, you two,' Michaela said to Yannick and Becca, 'why not do the event for fun — you're already tacked up and you're ready to go. I'm sure no one would mind that.'

Yannick seemed to disapprove of doing things just for fun, but Becca agreed heartily. 'Please, Yannick,' Becca wheedled. 'We may as well.'

'Fine,' Yannick said. 'Fine.'

'Great! Let's go down and have a look at the course together, shall we?' Michaela said.

Seeing the matter of the Jigsaw was resolved, Mrs Sand bellowed to Jade: 'Still keen to take Taniwha?'

Jade blushed from her neck up, seeing Michaela's face.

'What's this, Jade?' Michaela asked, incredulous.

'The girl with the broken foot offered to take Loretta's pony yesterday,' Mrs Sand announced. 'I just want to know if she's still interested. And, if so, whether you've room in your trucks to take him today.' Mrs Sand thumped Loretta's back. 'Don't start crying again, darling — you'll be better off without him.'

Michaela gave Jade a long, questioning look, then said with remarkable composure, 'Jade's father will here by lunchtime; perhaps we could discuss Taniwha then?'

'Alright,' Mrs Sand said impatiently, 'but we'll be leaving straight after the prize-giving and I'll want to know whether we're taking the brute with us or not.'

As she was no longer competing for points, Becca's nerves had left her. She was happy to walk the course with Yannick, and leave Michaela to have a frank discussion with Jade.

Having heard Jade's reasons for wanting Taniwha, Michaela sighed. 'Jade, just because the last pony you adopted turned out to be a good bet doesn't mean that this one will. Pip is bombproof and willing — a lucky find on your part. Taniwha, or whatever his name is, might be a nice, talented pony somewhere underneath all the fear and frustration he's developed with Sands. But even if he is, it will take a *long* time to bring him into his own. *Lots* of hard, patient work on your part. Shows, pony club — all those things that Pip does without turning a hair — would be a massive challenge with a pony like him.'

Jade nodded, thinking only about how nice it would be once Taniwha had settled down. She was patient; she could help him, couldn't she?

'Jade, are you listening to me?' Michaela snapped. 'Can you honestly tell me you'd rather go back to square one with a pony that broke your foot rather than buying an already proven pony? Sure, get something younger and greener than Pip, but not a pony that's been beaten up and confused.'

'But that's why I want him!' Jade argued. 'I want to help him.'

'It'll be years of hard work, possibly for little reward,' Michaela warned.

'I don't care.' Jade was uncomfortably aware that Kristen, Amanda, Corina and David seemed to be tacking up very slowly. Although they appeared to be doing up girths and threading reins through running martingales, Jade could tell they were listening.

'Have you called Mr White to ask if he'd mind an extra pony in his paddock?'

Jade was quick with her answer. 'Pip doesn't use the paddock anymore, so there's lots of room. And that Lisa girl had her horse, Floyd, there earlier this year.'

'And what about Pip?' Michaela continued. 'How will you cope with a troubled youngster *and* an ill old pony? Will you have time?'

'I'll make time!' Jade was almost shouting. 'Sorry, I just really want Taniwha.'

'Evidently,' Michaela said dryly. 'Look, let's wait until your dad gets here. If he lets you have the pony that broke your foot, call Mr White. If he agrees to graze the pony that broke your foot, I'll drive him home in our truck. Provided he loads! I can't be doing with a repeat of Medusa's drama.'

Jade frowned. It was more than likely that Taniwha

would cause problems in the truck. 'Dad won't agree to it unless you tell him it's a good idea.'

'I don't think it's a good idea; I think it's a gamble, and that you don't know what you're getting yourself into,' Michaela said, making Jade's face fall. 'But — wait, don't look like that — I'll also say that I think you could provide Taniwha with a much, much more capable home than the Sands. How's that?'

Jade grinned, seeing that Michaela had come around.

'I'd vouch for Jade,' Kristen piped up, unable to keep quiet any longer. 'It's not much different to Andy with her pony, Piper, and they're doing pretty well now. And remember when Johnny used to go berserk at shows? Taniwha's just green.'

'Well, the expert has spoken,' Michaela said. 'Jade, you have Kristen's blessing, for all it's worth.'

'Mum, I know what I'm talking about!' Kristen argued.

Jade grinned, relieved to no longer be the focus of the conversation.

Hobbling down to the junior ring to watch Becca and Yannick's round, Jade noticed a familiar white Falcon driving into the visitors' car park. Swinging herself over on her crutches as fast as she could, Jade met her dad just as he was hopping out of the car and stretching his legs.

'Dad!'

'The walking wounded!' he said. 'You're doing well on those crutches.'

When they'd hugged and made sure each other was alright — that Jade's foot wasn't too sore and that the drive hadn't been too stressful — Jade dragged her father to the junior ring.

As they approached the eastern side of the course, Jade could see Dusty racing at the rainbow triple bar. The back rail was at the full 90 centimetres, and he cleared it cleanly. Making a tight left turn as they landed, Becca stood in her stirrups, driving her pony on through the finishing flags with uncharacteristic aggression. Yannick was finishing simultaneously through the flags at the other end of the course.

'Was that Becca?' Jade's dad asked.

'Yep!' Jade said, excited.

'They looked very good.'

'It's a shame the points don't count because I reckon they'd have won,' Jade said, then explained the situation in full to her baffled dad.

'So you don't have to forfeit your points for the whole competition — it's just this round?' he asked.

'Yeah,' Jade said. 'We might still win if the others do well in the Jigsaw.'

As they walked over to congratulate Becca and Yannick on a good round, Jade decided that if she was going to ask her dad for Taniwha, it would be better to ask sooner rather than later. She didn't want Yannick blurting something out before she'd had time to bring her dad round to the idea gently.

'Dad, you know how Pip's never going to jump again?'

'Yes,' he replied slowly, having a good idea of what was coming.

'Do you think I could get another pony?'

'If you can look after it as well as you've looked after Pip, I don't see why not.' While Jade had been away, her dad had been discussing with Mr White the possibility of a new pony.

'What if it was the one that broke my foot?' Jade said, opting for the direct approach.

'What?'

Using all the arguments she'd tried on Mrs Sand, Mr Parry and Michaela, Jade bombarded her father with, in her mind, excellent reasons why they should take Taniwha back to Mr White's.

'So Michaela thinks it's a good idea?' her dad asked, when Jade had run out of words.

'Yes. And she said that if Mr White didn't mind grazing another pony, she'd be happy to take Taniwha in her truck.'

'Take him today?' her dad asked, aghast. 'Will he come with a coat and a saddle and so forth?'

'It's called a cover, Dad,' Jade laughed, but she didn't know the answer to his question. 'We can ask Mrs Sand soon.'

'And how much is he?' Jade's dad asked, bracing himself.

'Oh, he's free,' Jade said. 'Mrs Sand said she didn't want to be responsible for what he might do to me, so won't accept any money.'

'Wonderful,' her dad replied. 'We're buying — no,

being given — an equine thug. Are you sure about this, Jade?'

It was a silly question, really.

At the Sands' truck, Mrs Sand didn't seem remotely similar to the woman who'd kicked her pony in the stomach the day before. She was all politeness to Jade's dad, with Taniwha's registration papers and a pen all ready.

'And we'd like to buy Taniwha's cover and halter, too,' Jade's dad said, as if he were placing an order for fish and chips. 'What about the saddle, Jade?'

'Oh, the saddle's not for sale; I'm so sorry,' Mrs Sand apologized pleasantly. 'It's a brand-new Prestige Italia, and we're hoping it'll fit Loretta's next pony. We might even buy a pony to fit the saddle, rather than the other way around.' Mrs Sand laughed, but Jade thought she was probably serious.

'The halter's nothing special — you can have that. But shall we say $150 for the cover, and I'll throw in his travel sheet and boots, shall I? Maybe $200? They're all quite new and in perfect condition.'

'Considering we're not paying anything for the pony, $200 seems pretty reasonable,' Jade's dad said, getting out his cheque book. 'Before I write this, Jade, is there anything else you can think of? Will Pip's new bridle fit him?'

'Yeah, it should do,' Jade said, reaching out to stroke Taniwha's nose. He flicked his head away, nearly getting Jade in the chin. 'No, I think that's all we'll need.'

'Super!' Mrs Sand said girlishly. 'Deal done. You happy, Loretta? Taniwha's going to a lovely home.' Loretta nodded uncertainly.

'Do you want to take him now?' Mrs Sand asked, apparently anxious to be rid of him.

Jade and her dad weren't really in a position to lead a young pony and carry two covers and travel boots, so said they'd be back with reinforcements soon.

They found the rest of the team standing at the senior ring, waiting for David's and Corina's round. None of the previous rounds had been clear, so Michaela was urging her seniors to ride cautiously.

'How do you think they'll go?' Jade's dad asked Michaela.

'David will be fine; Corina and Medusa: who knows?' Michaela said. There were dark shadows under her eyes and it occurred to Jade what a long, tiring weekend it must be for the coach.

The bell rang, and Toblerone and Medusa both broke into a canter. As Michaela had predicted, David and Toby were making it look easy. Jade suddenly understood where the phrase 'taking it in his stride' came from. However, Corina and Medusa pulled out a surprising performance. The mare, who'd been nappy all weekend, finally had her ears pricked and was looking for the next jump rather than keeping one eye on the exit. Corina, too, who'd been dispirited since the unfortunate drive from Flaxton, had returned to her old competitive self.

'Did you finish before me?' David asked Corina, as they jogged out together.

'Yep, and clear!' Corina couldn't stop grinning.

'This is the perfect note to end on,' Michaela said, congratulating her eldest charges. 'I thought Amanda and Kristen did a good round, but that was *impressive*; and the first clear round, too! I'm delighted, I really am. I'm not at all nervous about hearing the results now!'

They didn't have to wait long for the results of the intermediate Jigsaw: Kristen and Amanda were second, right after Gorsewood.

As they did their lap of honour, the blue sashes complementing Johnny's coat and clashing with Blueberry Tart's, Jade thought Michaela was going to cry, she looked so proud.

'That girl's done wonders with Johnny,' Michaela said. 'Just as I expect you will with Taniwha, eventually. You've heard all about Jade's plan?' Michaela asked Jade's dad.

'Yes, the foot-breaker is now ours. Thanks very much for offering to taxi him home.'

'Anything for such a good little team member,' Michaela said, patting Jade's shoulder. 'You've done brilliantly this weekend, young lady — broken foot or not. It's just a shame you and Dorian couldn't have done the Jigsaw with Becca.'

'Do you know if they would have won?' Jade asked.

'Yep, their time was easily the fastest,' Michaela said, with some regret. 'Ah well, never mind. There's still a possibility of the cup being ours.'

The Flaxton team's chances were even better when the judge called David and Corina in first and tied a red sash around each of their horses' necks.

Weary from standing on one foot and clapping, Jade was glad to return to the trucks with the cavalcade of triumphant riders and ponies. There was just time to make the horses comfortable and the riders presentable before the prize-giving.

David, who was always the swiftest at untacking, had Toby fed and watered, and himself spruced up, before the girls had even finished unplaiting. Jade asked him if he'd mind leading Taniwha from the Sands' truck.

'I don't know,' he said. 'I'm not wearing my steel-cap boots.'

'I'm sure he'll be fine,' Jade said, sure of no such thing.

Fortunately, Taniwha was in fact quite docile as David led him, while Jade's dad carried the covers and boots and Jade went as fast as she could alongside on her crutches.

Feeling too scruffy to attend the prize-giving, Jade resisted the entreaties of her team-mates and opted instead to stay with Taniwha.

'It'll be dark when you get to your new home, mister,' Jade whispered, stroking the pony's lower neck and shoulder, having learnt that his head was, for now, out of bounds. 'But there'll be a friendly old pony there to keep you company, and two horses, and a nice man called Mr White. He'll know what to do with you if you're naughty — I hope.'

Jade's dad laughed, listening to his daughter chatting quietly away to her new pony. 'Will you be travelling in the truck with your new friend, or might you keep your father company in the old Falcon?'

'Oh, I'll come with you,' Jade said. 'So long as we stay close to the trucks.'

'As you wish,' her dad said.

Michaela's truck was first in the convoy, with a sizeable cup sitting on the dashboard — until it fell off and Kristen was told to put it on the floor. Despite their run of bad luck — Pip's lameness, Medusa's injured fetlock, Jade's broken foot — Flaxton had been the winning team at the New Zealand Pony Club Association North Island Show Jumping Championships. Gorsewood were, in the end, a close and relatively gracious second place.

Becca's truck followed the Lewises'. It was carrying Taniwha, whom Becca's mum had chosen over Medusa when she saw how well he was getting on with Dusty.

'I hate to be sexist,' she'd said, 'but I'd choose a gelding over a chestnut mare any day.'

Jade and her dad followed Taniwha. Jade tried to see through the truck's back wall and imagined her new pony standing side on, next to Dusty, hopefully scoffing his net of hay. No matter how slowly the truck went, Jade's dad wouldn't pass it.

'Thanks for coming to get me, Dad,' Jade said. 'I couldn't have stretched my leg out like this in the cab of the truck.'

Her dad was concentrating on the road, driving cautiously but seeming to enjoy it. 'Is it good to be back behind the wheel?' she asked.

'It was odd at first,' he said quietly. 'But now it is

good, yes. It feels like progress, somehow.'

Jade was slightly embarrassed at her dad's honesty. They were silent for awhile and Jade knew they were both thinking about her mum.

'Your mum would've enjoyed that show,' her dad said eventually, trying to sound casual. 'She would've been proud of you.'

Jade nodded, not feeling like speaking yet.

'Not sure if she'd have approved of this Taniwha, though.'

Jade laughed. 'Probably not. But I'll prove her wrong,' Jade said quickly, confusing her tenses. 'He's going to be great.'

With a broken foot, and an awfully late night unloading horses and unpacking tack, Jade thought it was reasonable to miss school on Monday. Becca, unsurprisingly, agreed. Her mum and Jade's dad seemed too tired to argue.

They parted quietly at Mr White's, after Becca had led Taniwha into the front paddock, taken his travel boots off and unclipped his lead rope.

In the middle of the night, after a long truck ride and with the smell of horses coming from the back paddock and the snickering of a pony coming from the yard, Taniwha was overwhelmed. After trotting in a couple of circles, he approached Pip, who was having her eyebrow scratched by Jade.

'This is your new brother, Pip; be nice,' Jade whispered, reaching out to Taniwha. He nosed her palm then pulled his head away and cantered down to the back fence to meet the others.

Over the phone, Jade had told Mr White about the new arrival. She hadn't thought it necessary to mention anything more than that Taniwha was a five-year-old bay gelding and a good jumper.

The next day, while, Jade calculated, Mr Wilde would be beginning a social studies lesson, Granddad, Holly and Jade drove to the Whites' to see how Taniwha had fared during the night.

Mr White was talking to Pip as they drove in.

'Just been discussing the new pony with the old lady,' Mr White said jovially. 'He hasn't broken any fences in the night, so we've agreed that he's welcome. How's the foot, Jade?'

'Itchy under the cast,' Jade said. 'I can't wait to get off these crutches, too.'

'You've got to be patient,' her granddad said, whistling at Holly. 'Oi, you little rascal — out of Pip's yard! She likes eating the horse poo.'

Jade made a face.

'Yes, I expect you're eager to start riding the new one; what's his name?'

'Taniwha,' Jade said slowly.

'And he's a good little jumper, you say? Might take you to the Champs again next year?'

'Um,' Jade paused. 'He *is* good at jumping, but he's a bit crazy. He's actually the pony that trod on my foot.'

'This sounds like it might be a long story,' Mr White said. 'Why don't you come in for some morning tea and you can tell me all about the little monster.'

Jade smiled, relieved; Mr White would understand.

'Holly!' Granddad called, opening the gate to Mr White's back garden. 'Come and have a bit of biscuit. Good girl!'

Sitting in the late summer sun on the back deck, listening to Mr White boiling the kettle and watching her old pony not just standing but moving of her own accord around the yard, Jade felt calm and happy. It was good to be home, with two ponies.

How to catch a pony

1. To prevent your pony from wandering off as you fumble with a tangled lead rope and buckles, make sure your halter is ready before going into the paddock. It is wise to have the nose-strap loosely buckled, the head-strap unbuckled, and the lead rope coiled tidily.

2. When your halter is ready, carry it in one hand behind your back, leaving your other hand free to hold out a titbit, such as half a carrot or apple. A whole carrot or apple will probably be too large for your pony to finish in one mouthful. If she drops the titbit and stretches her head down to eat it, you will have trouble pulling the halter over her nose.

Here is a trick for cutting an apple in half when

you don't have a knife handy: push the apple onto a fence until the wire cuts halfway into the flesh, then turn and push the apple against the wire until it falls into two halves.

(3) Once in the paddock (remember to close the gate!), with the halter behind your back and half an apple held out in front, call your pony's name. If she lifts her head from grazing, pricks her ears, whinnies and starts walking towards you, all well and good — keep walking and talking to your pony until she has taken the apple from your flat palm.

If she turns away, lays her ears back and flicks her tail as if a fly is tickling her hock, prepare to be patient. Keep talking softly, to let your pony know where you are, and remember to approach in a half-circle towards her left, or near-side, shoulder. If you walk straight to her head or tail, she won't see you until the last moment and may be alarmed. All going well, your pony's mood will improve once she finds the apple.

If, on seeing you, your pony is less placid and, for instance, trots in a large circle around you or canters to the far corner of the paddock, don't panic. Stand still, stop talking to her, even look away from her, but keep the treat held out. In this stance, you will become a curiosity, which, with a bit of luck, your pony won't be able to resist.

If, after a couple of circuits of the paddock, your pony hasn't been overwhelmed with curiosity and ventured over to take the apple, you may need the help of other people, ponies or treats. A stern adult standing in the corner where your pony usually flees to will make you and your apple more attractive. Catching your pony's paddock mate will often encourage your naughty pony to approach you willingly. If all else fails, a small bucket of hard feed placed in the paddock should prove enticing. Only use this final method if your pony appears to be genuinely timid, rather than just misbehaving, otherwise you will find that she becomes opportunistic and even more difficult to catch. If your pony enjoys being ridden and groomed, she shouldn't mind being caught either — in this case, a titbit is not always necessary.

(4) Now that your pony is eating out of your hand (or a bucket nearby), stand near her head, and reach gently around her neck with the lead rope until it is in a loop, with both ends in your hand under her neck. Holding the lead rope in one hand, so that your pony doesn't make a run for it before you've done up any buckles, slip the halter over the pony's nose. At this point, you can let go of the lead rope, reach under the pony's chin and flick the head-strap over behind her ears, ready to be buckled at her cheek.

(5) With half an apple in her stomach and the prospect of a ride, your pony should walk happily by your side back to the yard or fence post where you groom her.

Remove the lead rope from your pony's neck,

holding it quite firmly in your right hand while carrying the slack of the rope in your left hand. Be careful not to wind the rope around your wrist or fingers; if your pony shied, this could give you a nasty injury.

Try to walk at your pony's left shoulder. If she's pulling and trying to jog ahead, leaning your shoulder into her neck will help make your right arm stronger. At all times, be aware of where your pony's hooves are: she probably won't mean to stand on your foot, but accidents do happen. This is why it is sensible to always wear covered shoes, preferably boots, while handling your pony.